Immortal Voyage

by
C. G. Powell
Edits by
Liz Schulte
* * * * *

Published in the United States by Terra Stellar Press.

Immortal Voyage
Copyright 2012 by C. G. Powell

ISBN-13: 978-0615681269
ISBN-10: 0615681263

Book art-cover, photograph of girl by Christine Atkins, Model – Alexis Thomas, final design Christine Powell Gomez.

DEDICATION

This book is dedicated to my family. Alexis, Issabelle, and Hunter, thank you for cooking your own dinners and cleaning up after yourself so mom can write. And to my awesome husband, without your constant support this would still be just a dream. You are my world and I love you all dearly.

ACKNOWLEDGMENTS

Thank you for being there for me. Mom and Dad, your constant encouragement is my rock. Brian, if not for your ability to keep Billy occupied, I would not have gotten half of this book done. The IC, for your support and friendship, thank you for lighting the way.

Thank you, Misty, Olivia, Lisa, and Melissa for taking time to beta read for me. A special thanks to Tawdra and her very keen eyes, and Liz, the best editor ever. If not for your extraordinary ability to read my mind and make the story read the way I meant for it to read, this story would still be good, but you helped me make it awesome. Mandie, if not for your extraordinary ability to market and promote, I don't think this endeavor would be more than a well-loved hobby. I could never thank you enough for that...You are all awesome!!!

Chapter 1

"My Laird, the priestesses from Hy-Brasil are here," announced the young man, half out of breath from his jaunt across the grounds.

"Well, don't just stand there, lad, bring them here post haste," shouted Rowe, pacing the foot of his wife's bed.

As soon as the boy was out of earshot his wife, Mila, chastised, "Rowe! Must you scare the poor lad? You act as though this is the first time I have given birth." His tall, handsome figure moved back and forth in front of the hearth, casting a restless shadow across the room. His pacing and snippiness wore on her already frayed nerves. "You need to calm down."

He turned to look at her, worry written across his brow. "I'm sorry, but this birth is unlike your others. I have every right to be worried, especially now that the priestesses are here," he confessed, before walking to her bedside.

She winced as the muscles around her stomach contracted and let out a deep breath as it finished. "I can't be worried about what may or may not come to pass. We will only know when this child has been birthed; until then, I refuse to think of the worst. Plus, you do enough worrying for the both of us," she snorted, rubbing the once tense muscles on her belly.

"I wish you would have allowed me to take you to Hy-Brasil," he said, clasping her hand. "It would have put my mind at ease, Mila."

"You know why I refused. I would rather die than give up this child," she professed, squeezing his hand firmly.

"Don't say that," he whispered, bringing her fingers to his lips. "There is still the chance the priestesses will take the baby." He sat in the chair next to the bed and ran his fingers through his hair.

A light tap on the door redirected his attention. "Enter," he yelled from his chair. Two figures shrouded in cloaks stood in the doorway along with the lad he startled earlier. "Leave us." He waved off their escort.

The taller of the two pulled back her hood to reveal an unearthly beauty. Her long limbs moved with unnatural grace as she approached Rowe and Mila. "I understand your concern, but you know the deal. It would be unwise to leave a child here to be persecuted for being different," she said bluntly.

"Salima, there is no need to keep yourself masked—you are among friends," Rowe said to the priestess.

Salima's skin turned the color of the sky on a clear day and her eyes changed to those more reminiscent of a cat than human.

"I have no intention of going back on our agreement, and as per our contract, if the child's appearance is normal, it will remain with us," he cited.

Standing, he strutted to where the other woman stood. "And you are?"

The other figure stepped away from the closed door and removed her cloak, placing it on a nearby table. Unlike Salima, she was of normal stature and color. Her light blonde hair was pulled back from her young face and held in place with an ornate clasp. "I'm the priestess Var," she stated as she bowed her head briefly in respect. "King Varen sent me to ensure a smooth transition, regardless of which way it may turn out, and to help with the birth," she added in a soft, kind voice.

"How fares King Varen?" Rowe asked, rubbing the side of his temple to relax the tension in his furrowed brow. He footed back to Mila's side and clasped her hand.

"My king fares well and wishes you and your lady would visit again soon. He misses your company."

Mila's face contorted with pain as the next contraction engulfed her. She squeezed Rowe's hand until the pain subsided. "I don't think it will be much longer." She winced as she let go of his hand. "Go to the hall and make arrangements for the crowd who will come the moment it's born." She chuckled, recalling the masses who showed up for Halis' birth two years ago.

"I shall take my leave then." He kissed his wife one more time before making his way to a grand room with three large fireplaces that served as the meeting hall and kitchen for his clan. He sat on a stool next to the center hearth and watched the flames dance as his mind wandered. *Had this all been a mistake?* He looked back on his and Mila's decision to have this babe. But his thoughts were interrupted as he was joined by the cook who prepared the fire to make the morning's bread.

"How fares our lady?" she asked, adding wood to the under part of the smaller bread hearth near the kitchen.

"She fares well and is being attended by the priestesses from Hy-Brasil," he said to reassure her that Mila was in good hands.

"The clan noticed their arrival," she exclaimed as she continued to stack the wood. "The roar of the dragon they rode on woke the entire village as it lit up the sky with its fiery breath!" She accidentally dropped the piece of wood in her hand on the floor in her excitement.

"How do they expect me to keep things secret when they fly here on a dragon, I ask? So much for anonymity," he blustered before the cook could respond to his question.

The cook chuckled while climbing a ladder to the loft to retrieve flour and yeast. "Should I expect the whole clan for breakfast then?" she yelled down.

"Now that they know their lady is about to give birth, it is safe to assume we will be joined for breakfast." Rowe laughed.

"My Laird, we wish nothing more than the safe birth of a strapping son. We love your beautiful daughters, but fear without an heir the clan may become feudal once more."

He thought back to a conversation he had with his friend, Prince Sarik, son of King Varen, after the birth of his fourth daughter. *"You should bring your lady with on your next trip,"* said Sarik. *"We can make it so she bears only sons."*

"I'm not sure Mila would approve of your magic. Already she criticizes your ways," Rowe replied. At this moment he looked back with regret at Mila's decision. He hoped when he brought her to Hy-Brasil she would consent to Sarik's offer. Once there, it wasn't long before she became sympathetic to the plight of one of the races and insisted on helping their cause. Instead of an heir for Eir, she carried the child of a dying race.

Rowe's inability to produce a male heir caused tension among his clan, and with each passing year the discord grew. "I too hope she delivers a much needed son," he replied somberly to the cook.

Soon the other clan members began arriving; each helped ready the room or assisted with the cooking. The din of the bustle bothered Rowe, so he got up from his stool and walked into the hallway where he was met by Var.

"You are needed urgently," she whispered just out of earshot of the crowd gathering in the hall.

"Is, is Mila okay?" he asked, stuttering on his words, his heart racing as he followed Var back to his wife's chamber.

When they reached the outside of the door, Var hindered his entrance. "Your wife has delivered a daughter who looks very much like her mother." Var cast her eyes down as Rowe smiled with joy. "She bleeds out, my Laird, and I have neither the skills nor equipment to stop it."

His joyful moment turned to terror as the last of her words sunk in. Stricken with panic, he threw open the door and rushed to Mila's side. Tears flowed down his face as he looked at the pale figure of his wife.

"Rowe, promise me you will allow your daughters to marry for love," she whispered, her eyes struggling to stay open.

"Mila, you can't leave me," he stammered, his hand clasping hers.

"Promise me," she demanded in a quiet urgency as she closed her eyes for the last time.

"I promise," he cried, laying his head on her chest as the sound of her heart faded to nothingness.

After several minutes, the lusty sound of a baby's cry flooded the room. Rowe stood at the side of the bed as Salima handed him the baby. "She will have need of a wet nurse. Var has gone to the great hall to find one, and Sarik sends his congratulations and sympathy," she said as she re-masked her true form.

"Salima, what am I to do?" he sobbed as he lightly bounced the baby in his arm, attempting to quell her crying.

"You will do as you have always done, Rowe. Lead your people. They need a strong laird to keep them together. You have five healthy daughters, and someday they will marry and add sons to your house."

He took a deep breath to clear his mind. "You're right. I do have five healthy daughters.   The clan will mourn the loss of their lady, and I must stay strong for them."

A soft knock interrupted their conversation. Var returned with a young clanswoman who had recently bore a babe of her own. A tear rolled down her cheek as she looked to the bed where the laird's wife lay. Rowe handed her the child.

"I'm sorry for your loss, my Laird. She was a great woman and much loved." The woman lightly touched his arm. Var put her arm around the wet nurse's shoulder and walked her out of the room.

"I must tell the others before rumors begin to fly." He sighed before exiting the room accompanied by Salima. They walked to the great hall together, but Salima stopped at the doorway, allowing Rowe to make his way through the crowd on his own. Once he reached the far side of the room, he stood on a table and cleared his voice.

"This day brings great joy and sadness. Our lady has delivered a healthy daughter." He stopped for a moment to allow the cheering to calm down and to regain his strength. "It is with great sorrow I tell you the lady Mila has passed during childbirth." The room went quiet, save the soft sobs of the clan. Rowe stepped down from the table and was joined by his old friend Kale.

Kale was a strong, stout man; his dark hair and eyes made him mysterious and foreign looking to the rest of the clan. He was born to the unmarried weaver's daughter about the same time that Rowe was born. Kale's father was unknown, and soon after his birth, his mother married the miller. Rowe speculated for years that Kale's father might have been from Hy-Brasil, but any time Rowe mentioned it, Kale laughed.

"I'm sorry for your loss. I know Mila was your life." He put his arm around Rowe's back and walked him out of the room, so he could grieve in private.

"Thank you for your concern, Kale. I'll need your and Jaren's help with the precession to the sidhe during the winter solstice. There's not much time to plan, but she would have wanted to be buried there."

"Don't worry about the arrangements, Jaren and I will take care of everything. You have a new babe to worry about and girls who will need their father in the coming weeks." They walked to the private courtyard behind Rowe and Mila's bedchamber. A tall lanky man joined them, his red hair glowing like fire against the backdrop of the rising sun.

"My Laird, the priestesses have taken your lady with them. They shall bring the prepared body to the sidhe for burial during the solstice. The priestess Salima said she would return within the moon cycle to check on Jael." Jaren paused then raised his brow. "Who is Jael?"

"It appears the priestess has named my youngest daughter." Rowe grimaced as the confused look left Jaren's face.

"I hear it's Dar's wife, Ulla, who suckles the child. Jael will be as round and chubby as her own babes." Jaren laughed, attempting to make light of the situation.

"My only regret is I didn't force her to have the baby in Hy-Brasil. They could have prevented her death, and she would still be with me." He sighed, leaning against the retaining wall that surrounded the courtyard.

Kale snickered. "Forcing Mila to do anything was as easy as moving a mountain."

"Tell me, Kale, how is it the miller had such a beautiful, fiery, obstinate daughter?" A faraway look briefly showed on Rowe's face.

"She was more like our mother than her father would care to admit. And there isn't a man here who would have it any other way."

Rowe turned to his side, rested his elbow on the wall and placed his hand on his brow. He rubbed his fingers across his forehead to relieve the pain. "I feel like I've been gutted. How am I supposed to raise five daughters without her?" He looked to Kale and Jaren.

"You'll need to hire help for starters. Keep Ulla around as long as you can; she'll be a good influence on the girls. Fe would be more than happy to help. She always wanted a girl, and now she can have five," Kale answered.

"What about your boys, Kale, won't they need their mother?"

"Tam is old enough to go on the hunt with me, and Ugis, although young, keeps his grandfather company at the mill. It's safe to say they no longer need their mother's apron strings to hold onto. Fe has become melancholy since Ugis began going to the mill. Spending time with your little ones is exactly what she needs." Kale laughed.

Rowe let out a deep breath. "Thank you both for your help. It's time I talk to the girls and check on the baby. I was so upset I couldn't even tell you what color hair Jael has."

"Don't worry about your guests. I asked everyone to leave after their meal so you could have privacy," Jaren said as the three walked back to the great house.

Rowe stood by the door of his daughters' room; his eyes glassed over with the tears he refused to allow to fall. With one last sigh, he opened the door. Fe sat on the edge of one of the beds with Halis on her lap cradled by one arm and Wren crying in the other. Betta was in the middle of the floor fussing at Lenni who danced around singing. "When I grow-up I will ride the dragon to Hy-Brasil like momma."

Ulla sat in a chair on the far side of the chamber suckling Jael, whose bright red hair peeked out of the blanket wrapped around her. Rowe raised his brow at the chaotic scene. "This is going to be a long day," he mumbled, picked up Lenni and carried her to her bed.

*** ~~~ ***

The weeks passed quickly. It was two days until the solstice, and after walking for several, the clan finally made it to the burial site. The quartz facing on the large mound came into view sparkling in the sunlight. The clear sunny day was a farce to the bitter cold that seeped into their bones. Before long the men built a large bonfire and several small ones for cooking. As they settled, Rowe made his rounds to check on everyone. It had been 40 days since the death of his wife, and tomorrow he would lay her to rest—a task he hoped would ease his grief.

The sun would set in a couple of hours, and the clan needed shelter for the night. Rowe organized the erection of a large circular tent for the whole clan. By the time the tent was complete, the sun's last light faded to darkness. Inside the tent laid a long fire, and the clan's men sang and played games while the women cooked and talked amongst themselves. Rowe smiled at his people's resilience. It had been a long, arduous six-day walk from their land in Eir to the tomb, but none complained. Even now they made merry in spite of their aching feet and frozen fingers.

Kale walked to where Rowe stood gazing at the fire. "My Laird, Prince Sarik has arrived."

"I wasn't expecting him until tomorrow," he stammered as he stood up from the log by the fire.

"He's alone and wishes to speak with you," Kale whispered out of earshot of the others.

Rowe and Kale walked outside the tent. On the other side of the sidhe stood an imposing figure with raven colored hair that glistened in the moonlight. As the men approached, Rowe motioned for Kale to stay back and continued alone.

Sarik and Rowe clasped each other's arm, embracing as old friends. "Sarik, you're early, I didn't expected you until morn."

Furrowing his forehead, Sarik looked around then in a low voice said, "We need to speak in private, wave off your men and come with me."

Rowe raised his brow, but waved off his men and followed Sarik into the nearby woods. After several minutes they came across a field. In the center sat a sky ship from Hy-Brasil—or the great fire-breathing dragon as his people referred to it. Warm air hit Rowe's face the moment they entered the ship, a comfort he hadn't felt in a few days. He followed Sarik to a small room containing a table and a couple of chairs.

"What is this all about, Sarik?" Rowe settled into the cushioned chair across from him.

"It's about Jael. Salima would like to run a few test on her to make sure she is healthy. Although I'm a bit curious as to why she would want to run test on a human child." Sarik raised his brow then poured himself and Rowe a drink.

Rowe slouched in his chair debating whether or not to tell Sarik the truth of Jael's conception. "Did she mention anything else?"

"No. But I wonder if it has anything to do with the fact that Mila gave birth to a girl. I've never seen them screw-up a simple gender selection procedure." Sarik swallowed the entire glass of liquor he just poured.

"When did Salima want to see her?"

"After the ceremony, I'd like for you to accompany me back home. Salima will meet us there with Jael. It shouldn't take more than a couple of days." Sarik poured himself another drink.

"I only want what's best for Jael. She's more precious than life itself. I'll accompany you on one condition; regardless of your results, Jael comes home with me." Rowe eyed the glass of blue liquid in front of him.

Sarik shrugged his shoulders at Rowe's odd demand. "Done. I'll personally see to it she's allowed to go home." Sarik reached his hand out to shake Rowe's and bind the contract.

Rowe stood and shook Sarik's hand. "Now if you'll excuse me, I have a clan to tend to."

Sarik got up from his chair and walked over to a bench with woolen blankets stacked on it by the outer hatch. "I thought you might need these," he said, handing the blankets to Rowe. "If you need more, send Kale for them."

"Thank you, Sarik. When the cold seeps into your bones, you can never have enough blankets." Rowe stepped out of the sky ship and walked back to the tent with blankets in hand—an item he knew was of little value to Sarik, but would be a tremendous value to his people. He sent Kale back to the ship to retrieve the remainder.

The night proved to be colder than expected, and by morning he was glad to have the extra blankets for his people. Sunlight peeked into the tent through the cracks as the men added wood to the remaining coals of last night's fire. The women fetched water to make the morning meal, which consisted of grain cereal with honey and dried meats.

By late afternoon Prince Sarik and the priestesses made their way to the sidhe carrying a casket of rounded glass, its insides glowing a strange hue of blue. The curved quartz wall of the henge shimmered in the sun's last light like tiny stars across the front of the massive mound it covered. The clan gathered around the front of the mound and waited for the ceremony to begin as Rowe joined Sarik and the priestesses. Looking into the casket, Rowe saw Mila lying there as if she were sleeping. The strange blue light shrouded her body with its eerie glow giving the appearance of divineness. He placed his hand on the casket and stood there. His mind drifted into a haze as if he were in a dream. The blue light blinded his senses to where he could no longer see or hear the things around him, leaving him in a state of nothingness as the cold embraced him. Var gently placed her hand on his. Her touch was like lightning coursing through him and waking him from his trance.

"It's time to lay the body to rest," she whispered as she let go of his hand.

Darkness had fallen and torches surrounded the clan; confused by his loss of time, Rowe mindlessly followed behind the casket into the tomb. Once inside, they walk along a large corridor until they reached an arched nook in the wall. The priestesses opened the casket and laid Mila's body in the nook.

"It is done," Rowe said as he turned and walked out of the crypt, just as the sun turned the sky red with light.

Chapter 2

17 years later- Summer Solstice

"Jael, they're here!" shouted Halis from the window. Laughing and grabbing Jael's hand, they ran to the courtyard to greet their older sister, Wren, and her husband, Dugun.

It had been five years since Wren married and two since her last visit. Her eyes were sunken within her gaunt face as the once vibrant beauty entered the courtyard. Dugun was a stout fellow with light brown hair and a ruddy complexion and had a demeanor of arrogance and self-importance only the son of a laird could have. He was the second son of the laird of Canulis and believed it was his right to rule Eir as Wren's husband if anything should happen to Rowe—an argument that caused Wren to be separated from her clan for two years. Dugun was the last person Rowe wanted for his daughter. He long hoped to marry her to Tam, the eldest son of Kale, but he promised he would allow his daughters to marry for love. Wren and Tam grew-up together like brother and sister. Before Wren could have romantic notions towards Tam,

Dugun enticed the girl with travel and a large home of her own—something Tam could not offer. Wren fell for Dugun the moment she laid eyes on the handsome warrior; his muscular body more than made up for his rather common face, and his way with words could make any maiden swoon. Rowe knew Dugun was a cruel man. He saw the way he treated the other members of his clan and tried to talk Wren to her senses, but the girl would have none of it. Now, five years later, Wren was wife to a heartless, self-centered man who thought of nothing but gaining power.

Jael and Halis threw their arms around Wren who was more like a mother than a sister to them. Wren was ten when their mother died, and as the oldest, she helped care for her younger sisters: Betta, eight; Lenni, seven; Halis, two; and Jael had just been born.

Jael pulled away from the embrace. "Why must you keep away from us for so long?" she asked, mouth tugged down and lower lip pursed over her top one.

Wren's eyes filled with water. "There are things you do not understand, things I can't control."

Halis rolled her eyes and chirped, "You mean things like that big oaf you call a husband?"

"Shush, young lady, he might hear you! I don't want to be dragged away from here again, so be nice to the oaf," Wren chastised, hugging the two girls again.

The girls walked into the house, bypassing the great hall where Dugun blustered and went to the large room where they slept together as children. Wren sat on the bed that was once hers—a pallet of straw covered in wool that lay on the floor. It was not the most comfortable bed in the world, but it was hers. She smiled as she listened to Halis and Jael chatter before asking, "Where is Lenni?"

"Our dear sister visits Betta and Haro. They're expected tomorrow for the clan meeting," answered Jael, gazing out the window at the people buzzing about the courtyard.

"I wish you could've been here for Betta's wedding. It was the most beautiful wedding, and Haro is certainly easy on the eyes." Halis giggled, skipping across the room towards Wren.

"And as dumb as a rock." Jael turned away from the window and walked to the pallet where Wren sat.

"Halis, Jael! You should not talk of your brother-in-law in such a way," Wren reprimanded before laughing.

"You'll see, Wren, when they get here tomorrow. Haro is the most handsome man you've ever laid eyes on." Halis sighed, fluttering her hand over her heart and looking up dreamily at the ceiling.

"Oh, I've missed you two so much. I wish I could stay in Halor forever." Wren clasped her sisters' hands with a wistful expression from the edge of the pallet. The cold seeped in through the open window, she shivered, breaking her melancholy thoughts. "It's chilly in here. Why is there no fire in the hearth?" she asked, pointing to the ash filled fireplace.

"I'll take care of it," Jael volunteered, getting up from the pallet and piled the logs on the inside of the hearth.

Wren stood to help; she looked around then asked, "Where is the kindling and flint?"

"Jael does not need them to start the fire," Halis announced as if it were common knowledge.

"What do you mean?"

Halis grinned from ear to ear. "Just watch," she said.

Jael placed her hand on top of the bottom log, closed her eyes, and concentrated. Within seconds the log burst into flames.

Wren jumped back. "How did you do that?" Her voice crackled as her heart beat in her throat.

"I'm not sure. All I have to do is think about it and the fire is there," Jael replied, shrugging her shoulders.

"Does father know?" asked Wren, furrowing her brow.

Jael looked at Wren and rolled her eyes. "Of course he does, and so does Salima, but they told me to keep it secret. Father fears if word got out, the other Lairds would try to steal me and use me as a weapon of war."

"And what of love, Jael? Will you not tell the man you marry?" asked Wren touching Jael's arm.

"Ha, Jael get married? She spends all of her time with father seeing to the clans' needs. She is like his shadow; he even includes her in negotiations with the other clan lairds," Halis chimed in.

"You make it sound as if it were a bad thing to learn how to lead." Jael shook her head.

Wren let out a huff, put her hands on her hips and paced the room. "Dugun thinks it's his place to lead this clan, and if he finds out Jael's being trained, he'll fly into a fit of rage and forbid me to see you again." Plopping on the bed she grunted loudly.

"My poor sister, we can't help that your husband has the temperament of an enraged stag." Halis laughed. "Besides, Jael cannot rule Eir without a husband, and with her lack of interest in men, it wouldn't surprise me if she never marries," Halis said, poking fun at her sister.

"Really, Halis, just because I don't flutter my eyelashes at every warrior who shows up on father's doorstep doesn't make me a spinster. I feel that one of father's daughters should learn to lead this clan," Jael ranted, closing the shutters on the windows.

A loud knock on the door interrupted their conversation. Wren peeked out to see who it was, and before her stood Tam, taller and more handsome than she remembered. His beautiful, green eyes were wrinkled around the edges, most likely from laughter, and a shadow of a beard accentuated his strong jawline. Wren stared for a moment before Tam interrupted.

"Hello, Wren, it's been too long since your last visit," he smiled as he lifted her hand to his lips.

Stunned, Wren opened the door all the way and took a step back. "Did you need something?" she asked nervously, breaking the spell between them.

"Oh...yes, I have a message for Jael. Your father needs you in the great room; the meeting is about to begin," he said. He looked back to Wren and grinned before making a slight bow with his head and walking away.

"Duty calls," said Jael as she followed Tam out the door and down the hall.

Wren stood motionless staring at the door as if she had seen a ghost.

"What was that all about?" clamored Halis as she took the door out of Wren's hand and closed it.

Wren shook her head and walked near the fire. "I don't know what came over me." She sighed, warming her hand near the flames.

"Well, I have an idea—I think you still love him," she blurted out, giggling as she joined Wren in front of the fire.

"Don't say that, Halis. Dugun would kill Tam if he caught him so much as looking at me." Wren stared into the fire so Halis could not see the tears that were threatening to fall.

"You're not denying my claim, so it must be true." Halis laughed, nudging Wren with her elbow. "I wish you had married Tam then I could see you every day."

"Me too." Wren put her arm around her sister's shoulder and pulled her close.

~~~

The room went quiet as Jael stepped into the great hall and Rowe motioned for her to join him. She looked around at the many men in attendance. All eyes followed as Jael's tall, graceful body crossed the room. Her hair was the color of flames and glowed against her pale translucent skin, and her eyes were as golden as the sun. Her appearance of etherealness almost begged to be worshiped, but Jael was oblivious to all of it. Rowe cleared his throat and the chatter that was there before Jael's arrival resumed.

"Father, why are there so many men from our neighboring clans?" she whispered in his ear.

Reading the confusion on her face, Rowe answered, speaking freely from the more isolated area of the room behind the dais. "I still have three daughters who have yet to take a husband and two unsuitable son-in-laws. I have left the clan without heir for too long, Jael, and I'm hindered by your mother's last request to allow you to marry for love. With so many to choose from, I hoped at least one of you might find a suitable husband among them."

"Then why have you only called me to this meeting?" she asked, cocking her head to the side giving her father a lopsided grin.

"Today we're to talk business, which is of little concern to Halis. She'd quickly get bored and distract everyone," replied Rowe as he showed Jael to her seat.

"I cannot disagree with that." She laughed as she took her seat.

The benches and tables were arranged so everyone faced the small platform where Rowe, Jael, and other prominent members of their clan sat along with the lairds of Canulis, Monmalor, and Hem. "Welcome to Halor, Lairds, honored guests, and friends. I thank you for making the journey across

Eir to discuss trade agreements, land settlements, and alliances. I hope all will leave with a sense of accomplishment at the end of the meeting, regardless of how much blustering goes on to reach our goals." He smiled as the crowd laughed and clapped. "So without further ado, I would like to start with our first issue, unprotected shipping routes along the southern coast...."

It didn't take Jael long to notice Dugun seething from a table below the dais. His scathing stare at her father sent a chill down her spine. The way he composed himself this evening, arms crossed and lips pursed as he rolled his eyes at every word Rowe said, left a bad taste in her mouth.

When his eyes made contact with her, Jael knew she was the source of his aggravation. Pure hatred and contempt radiated from his leer, but Jael refuse to look away as she sat up straight in her chair in defiance.

~~~

The meeting continued until hunger won out, and the men were joined by their women in the great hall for supper. Music and laughter filled the air as tempers calmed and made light of the festivities. Jael was glad to be joined by Halis and Wren as her father introduced a long line of men, which Jael had no interest in. Halis, on the other hand, enjoyed the attention. Eir was one of the richest lands around, so many suitors came to meet the girls. The capitol city of Halor served as the sole port for the western side of the island and was a prize worth winning. Marriage to any of Rowe's daughters was a great bounty for any man. Jael looked for a way out of her father's man trap when she spotted Tam by the fire. She broke free from the crowd of suitors clamoring to speak with her and made her way to Tam.

"I see your father is beginning to feel his mortality and has pressed the marriage issue again." He laughed at the exasperated expression on Jael's face.

"It's not funny, Tam." She grinned as she nudged him with her elbow.

"I'm sorry, Jael. You know he only does what he thinks is best."

"I know, but could he be more obvious about it? And what about you, Tam? I don't see everyone scrambling to get you a wife. Not that they would have to look far as handsome as you are. You already have the lady folk swooning over you," she teased as she smiled.

"Alas, my heart was broken the day Wren married. I shall never find an equal love, so I'll live my life in solitude for all eternity," Tam dramatized, as if he were being stabbed in the heart.

"Awe....my poor Tam. How disappointing you should exile yourself when my father wishes for nothing more than your marriage to one of his daughters—any of his daughters," she added stoically, before laughing.

"Is that a proposal, Jael?" Tam teased.

Straight-faced Jael answered, "Yes, Tam, I'm confessing my undying love for you. Marry me before my father throws another man in front of me." She rolled her eyes and laughed.

"Thank you, Jael, now I have been jilted by two of Rowe's daughters. You ladies bring me nothing but pain," he said, clasping his hand over his heart.

Jael let out a big belly laugh. "I'm sorry, Tam, but our ten year age difference and your undying love for my sister prevents me from loving you as anything more than a beloved brother."

He reached out and clasped her hand. "And you, my dear, are the sister I never wanted." He chuckled, before kissing her hand.

"Speaking of sisters, I should check on Halis before she charms herself into something she'll regret later," Jael said.

"Until we meet again, my lady Jael," Tam said, bowing then taking his leave.

Jael made her way around the room; she craned her neck looking for Halis and Wren, but when she could not find them in the great hall she searched the house. Walking passed the room where Wren and Dugun lodged, she heard Dugun yelling.

"Why does your father put Jael above me?" he screamed. "He allows her to participate in negotiations as a man would a son, and I find it intolerable. This is your fault, Wren."

Jael winced as she listened to flesh hitting flesh and the sound of her sister crying, begging his forgiveness. The whole event sickened Jael. She walked away from the door and out to the private courtyard, where she leaned against the wall and exhaled deeply, trying to calm her nerves. *What should I do?* She thought. *If I tell father, Wren will be dragged away again, and if I tell Tam, a fight would ensue which could lead to a war between clans.* Jael needed to talk to someone, someone who could stay neutral. As if on cue, Salima joined Jael at the wall.

"What troubles you, my child?" she asked.

Jael was always astounded by how Salima knew when she was troubled. "I heard an argument between Wren and Dugun. He said I shouldn't be allowed to attend the negotiations and that father should put him before me. Then he hit Wren and said it was her fault," Jael blurted out nervously.

"That's troubling indeed. And if you were a leader, what would you do?" Salima questioned, expecting Jael to find her own answer.

"I can't go to father, that would cause a bigger rift and we may never see Wren again. If I tell Tam, he and Dugun will

fight and most likely start a war. Either way Wren loses."
Taking a deep breath of the lavender-filled air she exhaled and
released the furrow across her brow.

"So what action would you take?"

"For now, I can refrain from going to further meetings and
give Dugun a sense of security. I should keep quiet about the
fight, so I don't stir up trouble. Father will always include me
in these matters, whether or not I personally attend the
meetings, and what happens between me and father when
Dugun is not here is our business, not his. In a nutshell, I
don't want to give Dugun a reason to lash out at Wren, but I
won't be bullied into abandoning all clan business," Jael
reasoned.

"Your father has always been aware of Dugun's cruelty,
and if not for the promise he made your mother, he would
never have agreed to let them marry. He doesn't agree with
the way Wren is treated, but he knows now is not the time to
strike," Salima explained.

Jael leaned over and hugged Salima. "Thank you, you
always know the right questions to ask."

"A lesson I'm glad is not lost on you." Salima laughed.
"I'll help you find Halis."

Jael looked at her in surprise. "How did you know I was
looking for her?"

"One day, Jael, I'll be free to tell you all of my secrets.
Until then, we'll just consider it a good guess." Salima smiled
before they walked back to the great hall.

They passed Tam and his brother Ugis who were leaving
to go home. "Have you seen Halis?" Jael asked.

"She's in the great hall surrounded by men," Ugis said
with a defeated frown.

"Thank you," Jael said, leaning over and kissing his cheek.
"Have a safe walk home," she added as they walked away.

Jael and Salima headed straight for the great hall. "It's a shame Halis does not feel the same way for Ugis that he feels for her. They'd be great for each other. He's overly focused, and she's not focused at all. Oh well, there's always Lenni," Salima teased as they looked around the room.

Just as Ugis said, Halis was surrounded by men and reveling in the attention. Rowe kept his distance as always— not by choice, but by promise. Jael padded to where her father spoke to Dugun's father, leaving Salima to keep an eye of Halis. Rowe stretched out his hand to her and kissed her cheeks. "How's my lovely daughter doing this night?" he asked.

"All is well, my Laird. I had to get some fresh air before returning to the festivities," she lied.

"Are you enjoying yourself, Lady Jael?" asked the Laird of Canulis.

"Yes, my Laird Canulis. In fact, I've come to let my father know I'll be spending the day with my sisters tomorrow and not attending his meetings as they're for the men," she said.

Her father raised a brow. "Very well, my child, enjoy your time with your sisters."

She made a slight bow and excused herself to join Salima and Halis. Jael conversed with few of the men surrounding Halis, but gave no impression that she was even remotely interested. After a few minutes, Jael dragged Halis away, insisting they needed their beauty sleep. As they walked to their shared room, the sound of Wren crying filled the hallway. Jael and Halis knocked on her door. Dugun's heavy footsteps approached the door before he flung it open. "What do you want?" he thundered, causing Halis to jump back from fright.

"We're wondering if you would be so kind as to let our sister sleep with us this night. I'd like to spend the entire morrow with her without disturbing you," Jael requested kindly.

"Are you not attending the negotiations?" he asked sarcastically.

"Why would I? They're for the men folk, and I'd prefer to spend my time with my sister," she replied.

"It matters not to me. By all means take her away, I was heading back to the party anyway," he said, storming out the door and down the hallway.

Wren threw her arms around her sisters and whispered, "Thank you."

~~

Betta's husband Haro stood alone near the large hearth of the great hall. Many of the guests had left for the evening, including Dugun's father. Haro waited patiently for Dugun. They had business to discuss, but the hall was not private enough for their conversation. As soon as Dugun returned to the party, they left for a small camp just outside the boundaries of Halor.

"You need to be more careful, Dugun. Your treatment of Wren will not win you any friends among the clan," reprimanded Haro.

"What about you? Did you not think everyone would notice you didn't bring Betta with you? Besides, I could care less what they think of me. Wren is only a means to an end and needs to learn her place," Dugun blustered.

Ignoring Dugun's questions, Haro fisted his hands at his side. "If you continue on this path, it will not matter that you are the husband of Rowe's oldest daughter. The clan knows Rowe has been grooming Tam since birth to take his place," Haro pointed out. "You need to win these people over if you plan on ruling them."

"Or get rid of Tam," Dugun snarled.

Haro let out a deep breath and unclenched his fists. It was quite apparent his request for restraint was lost on Dugun. "Only if you want to find yourself at war with Eir, which, at the moment, is not an option," Haro stated.

"I grow tired of your caution, Haro. I'd rather march my army across Eir and be done with it than spend another day kowtowing to Rowe's disrespect."

Shaking his head, Haro sat down on a nearby stone and stretched out his legs. "There are things about Rowe you don't understand. He has a secret ally who could destroy an army in seconds. Only a fool would challenge him. No, Dugun, war is not an option—at least not a winnable one. We need a precision attack and Rowe is the link. With him gone, we can remove his ally from the equation, but now is not the time. You need to exercise patience and have an army ready before this plan can move forward."

"What about you, Haro? What's your contribution to this plan?" Dugun asked sarcastically.

"I have my own agenda, none of which is your concern. Do not do anything stupid in the meantime or you may find yourself dealing with more than a disrespectful wife," warned Haro.

Haro's threat sent a chill down Dugun's spine.

C.G. Powell 26

Chapter 3

By week's end, the talks concluded and the guests made their way back home. Lenni, Halis, and Jael sat in the great hall and awaited their breakfast.

"What a long week. I'm glad to have seen Wren, but I could do without her husband. And I wish Betta had come; Haro made me nervous the whole ride here," complained Lenni.

"I thought you liked Haro. Is that not why you went to visit?" teased Halis. "And did you not enjoy the company of the men father invited?" She grinned at her sisters from ear to ear.

"Haro may be handsome, but he scares me. The whole time I was visiting Betta, I felt as if a demon were watching me," Lenni glowered. "And you know my heart is elsewhere, Halis. I'll not be happy until I find *him*," she retorted as she poured a cup of goat's milk.

"Do you truly believe he's real, this man who haunts your dreams?" Halis asked, leaning forward in a whisper, as if he were a ghost listening to their conversation.

"He has to be. I've seen his face a thousand times, and every time I look into the eyes of another man, he appears in my mind," Lenni confessed as the cooks brought sweet breads and honey to the table.

Jael reached for a roll and slathered it in honey, paying no mind to her sisters' mindless chatter. Now that Dugun was gone it would be business as usual. She had much to talk about with her father; although he was disappointed she did not attend the negotiations, he conceded to her wish once she explained the reason. The meeting appeared to be a complete success, even down to finding at least one of his daughters a suitor. Halis had taken an interest in a young man from Monmalor just as the talks were ending, and he promised to return as soon as he could. He was a horseman, and her father offered to build him a fine stable for his beasts if he taught him how to ride. In all honesty, Jael believed it was just a way for him to keep his daughter near, and although Edric was a hard worker and honest man, he was not laird material. Once more, Rowe would be left wanting of a worthy son, and with only two daughters left, he was beginning to lose hope.

The girls craned their necks at the sound of the hall door creaking open. "Jael, there you are. I wanted to sit down with you today and discuss the negotiations. When you're done, can you meet me in my private chamber?" Rowe asked his daughter as he grabbed a plate of food and left before Jael could answer.

Halis flashed Lenni a lopsided grin and raised her brow. "So, Lenni, are you planning to go to Wren's to look for your dream man?"

"Honestly, Halis, must you continue to pry?" she asked, already annoyed with the constant questions. "I have no intention of one spending even one day under Dugun's roof, not even for Wren's sake. Besides, he has hair black as a raven's feathers and eyes as blue as the summer sky and this is not common to the men around here, so I'll wait for him to come to me," Lenni prattled almost dreamily, forgetting her previous irritation.

"Ooh...Sounds exotic, I can't wait to meet him too," squealed Halis as she rolled her eyes sarcastically.

"You're such a baby, Halis," Lenni snapped, lips pursed and eyes squinted as if to kill.

"You won't think so when I marry before you and your imaginary man," Halis retorted, sticking out her tongue.

"All I can say is: welcome home, Lenni. I've missed your ability to entertain Halis with endless nattering, so I'm able to attend to other business," Jael said sarcastically as she got up from the table and left the room. She walked down the hall to her father's private room; it was not large as the other rooms in the house were, but it was cozy. Its walls were covered in beautiful dark wood with carved ornaments in each corner, and unlike the wooden floors of the rest of the house, his was made of polished stone that glistened in the firelight. The chairs in this room had backs and arms to them and covered cushioned seats, something she had seen nowhere else.

"Jael, I wish you would've attended the meetings with me. I could've used your council—you have a peculiar way of looking at things—but I understand the issue with Dugun. Sometimes I wish he would fall off of his stag pony and break his neck!" Rowe exclaimed, banging his fist on the table.

"Calm down Father. Dugun will get what he deserves. Until then we must wait." She touched the top of his fisted hand and gave him a half grin, hoping to make his anger wane.

"That boy will be the death of me, Jael, then what will happen to the clan?" He sighed and ran his fingers through his hair before placing his hands on the table and taking a deep breath.

Jael sat in the chair across from him, reached out, and clasped his hands. "You're far from having one foot in the grave, Father. Plus, I'll always be here for our people. You went through great lengths for us this week. It could not have been easy to assemble so many young men and I want to thank you. I know it seems that I'm disinterested, but the fact is none of them were the right one for me. I hope you understand and are not angry," she explained, trying her best not to upset him.

"You of all people should know that I will love you no matter what you choose." Rowe gave her hands a squeeze then released them.

"Now, back to the subject at hand. The Laird of Hem has offered soldiers to help guard the southern coast; in return we will allow his people to settle in the area of Eir adjacent to Hem. His lands lack a suitable area to grow grain for mead, and as part of this arrangement, Eir seamen will transport the extra mead along trade routes, splitting the profits with Hem," Rowe explained as best as he could remember.

Jael pursed her lips and waited a second to think before replying. "What time constraints have you given them?"

Leaning back in his chair, Rowe let out a deep breath. "I had not thought to put a time limit on the arrangement," he replied in earnest, peeved at his own oversight.

"By setting a time limit, we can assure that all lands are reverted back to Eir for renegotiation and prevent the property from becoming assimilated by Hem in the future—long after this agreement is forgotten," she reasoned, a skill Salima taught her at a young age.

Rowe shook his head. "This is the exact reason why I needed you at these talks. Thankfully nothing has been finalized; I will add time frame to the contract before we meet in six months to finalize the deal." He sighed. "Dugun will not be attending, so I fully expect you to be there," he commanded, shaking his finger at her.

"Yes, my Laird," she answered in a business-like tone as a retort to her chastising.

"Now, the next item I need your input on is trade with Monmalor. As you know, Monmalor is land locked which makes trade beyond its neighbors difficult, so it was proposed a neutral trade route to the sea be established following the river west. I have offered to share our eastern port because it could use the added protection Monmalor and its horses will bring. Plus, it will give my merchant ships some added trade as Monmalor's boats are too small to make the voyage across the sea." He paused thumbing through the parchments in front of him. "Did you see the handsome animals they brought with them? You should have seen the look on Dugun's face when they arrived on stag ponies, it was priceless. With the addition of Edric to the family, Halor will have its own stable of fine horses and an equally competent horse master," Rowe smiled, proud of his achievement of finding Halis a suitable husband.

"But not an heir," Jael inserted matter-of-factly.

"I'm afraid the task of protecting the borders and negotiating trade is too complex for him, and he is merely nineteen. He would be no match for Dugun," Rowe deducted.

"Maybe he can learn as I did. You and Salima are the best teachers one could ask for."

"We shall see. Maybe even Tam can help him. He would have been a strong leader for our clan had your sister married him. I saw you talking to him at the gathering and thought there might be something going on between you two—or just an old man's wishful thinking," he hinted.

Jael's face turned red as she exclaimed, "Father! You know Tam is ten years older than me and like a brother. I could never marry him, not even for you." She laughed, trying to make light of her father's suggestion.

"We plan to gather here again during the winter solstice in six months. If all goes well, Halis will marry Edric at that time. Before then, I have some business to take care of in Hy-Brasil. Wren and Dugun have volunteered to stay and take care of things. Truthfully, I would rather have left Kale in charge, but I feared what Dugun might do if he found out. In the meantime, I expect you to have contracts drawn up and ready for our winter gathering. Which reminds me; we received a pack of parchment and two bales of wool from Hem today as payment for the two parcels of fabric we sent home with them. I must remember to thank the weaver as they were most impressed by her work," he added.

"Can I go to Hy-Brasil with you?" she asked nervously. Ever since she was a child she heard stories of the mysterious island shrouded in mist.

"Jael, if I could, I would take you. But permission from King Varen is required and not often granted. If it will make you happy, I will ask while I'm there, so you may go next time." Sooner or later he was going to have some explaining to do; he hoped it would be later. Unfortunately, as Jael's powers grew, he realized that she might need to be sent there to learn to control them—a thought that saddened Rowe.

Jael's face lit up as she threw her arms around him and laughed. "Thank you, Father."

"Jael, just because I have said yes, does not mean that Varen will."

"I know, but at least you will ask if I can accompany you next time and that makes me happy to know there is a chance I may get to go."

"Now, back to business. Laird Canulis is having problems with the barbarians that plague the lands south of his. Canulis is the only thing that stands between the civilized clans and those demons. He proposed forming a permanent army made up of men from all of the northern lands to protect the southern border. All have agreed, with the exception of Hem who has already volunteered to supply men and boats to guard the coastal areas with my men and a couple of boats from

Canulis. One day we will have to go on the offense and rid ourselves of this wolf at our back."

"A joint army is a great idea. I know you have always dreamed of consolidating the northern lands."

〜〜〜

The summer passed and so had Jael's seventeenth birthday before Rowe made his way to Hy-Brasil a month before the winter solstice. He planned to go sooner, but clan business and unusually rough seas kept him from going. Rowe nervously waited for the sky ship to land; he did not like to fly, but travel by boat at this time of year was dangerous so he took Sarik's offer. Upon his arrival in Hy-Brasil, Rowe was met at the landing area by Sarik. They walked along the paved streets until they reached a house that contained a large room and several smaller ones. At the end of the hall they entered a room containing a table with one chair behind it and two in front. The walls were covered in glass and metal, but the floor was covered in polished stone similar to what Rowe had in his private chamber. The men sat down across from each other and engaged in idle chit-chat before getting down to the real reason for Rowe's visit.

"Sarik, I need your help. My clan is falling apart because of a promise I made seventeen years ago. Wren's husband is a cruel, power-hungry man, and if I don't find at least one suitable husband among my daughters who can take on Dugun and win, all will be lost. I have given this much thought, and among my daughters, the only one capable of running the clan is Jael." Rowe paused before continuing. "I only ask this because I know of your immortality and reasoned that thirty years or so of your life to help a friend would be inconsequential," he blurted out as he dropped to his knees from his chair.

Sarik furrowed his brow as he listened to Rowe's plea. "Get up. You know I'll help you in any way I can, so there's no need to beg. Now, what exactly do you need of me?" he asked calmly.

Rowe took a deep breath and paused for a second. "I want you to marry Jael and become my heir."

Sarik sucked in a large breath of air and coughed uncontrollably as his face turned red. Rowe rushed to his side and patted him on the back until he regained his composure. Sarik wiped the tears from his eyes with the palms of his hands, then apologized for his reaction. "I did not see that coming," he croaked.

"I know it is a lot to ask, Sarik, but my back is up against the wall. Jael is a beautiful, smart woman—a prize to any man lucky enough to win her."

Sarik let out a sigh. "I do not doubt her beauty or worth, Rowe. I hadn't contemplated a proposal of betroth. How does Jael feel about this?" he asked.

"I didn't ask her. It breaks my heart just thinking about it. Of all my daughters, she is the one who deserves love the most, and I am about to break my promise and take that away." Rowe placed his elbows on the table and face in his hands.

"I need time to think. Marriage is something I had not considered. And to be honest, I rather enjoy my freedom," Sarik said bluntly as he leaned back in his chair.

"I will understand if you decline, and your answer will have no effect on our friendship. Please take whatever time you need," said Rowe as he got up from his chair to leave.

"No need to leave, old friend. Please, stay and enjoy a couple of days here before you return. I could use your company. Father has been on a mission to get me to take things more seriously, and it's depressing."

Stopping at the door, Rowe turned around on his heel and returned to his seat. "Maybe your father is right, Sarik. A wife just might be what you need to get him off your back." Rowe laughed.

〰〰〰

It was the morning of the winter solstice and the great hall was abuzz with excitement. Holly and juniper boughs draped across the wall with bouquets of dried lavender hanging between them. Breads, dried fruit, and cheeses sat on every table awaiting the festivities of the evening. In their childhood room, Jael and Lenni helped Halis into her gown while Fe and Salima chatted by the hearth.

Jael raised her brow at Halis being unusually quiet. "Are you okay?"

Halis inhaled a ragged breath then let it out. "I'm a little nervous," she replied before she paced like a caged animal. "Why am I nervous? I love Edric; he makes me happy. I shouldn't be nervous. But what if he takes me away from my home or turns into an ogre like Dugun? What am I getting myself into?" Her voice became shrill as she gazed at Fe. She placed her hands over her chest as if to quell the pain that was building from her rapid breath. Fe rushed to over to Halis and put her arm around her waist.

"Lenni, loosen her dress laces," Fe commanded. She walked Halis over to the window and threw open one of the shutters as Lenni shuffled behind them and pulled the strings on the back of Halis' gown.

"Take a deep breath. Edric is a kind man and would never treat you as Dugun treats Wren." Fe looked back at Jael who was still standing in the middle of the room a bit miffed by the whole event. "Please fetch Halis a cup of wine." Fe snapped her fingers at Jael to get her attention.

Jael nodded and dashed out the room.

Halis hung her head outside the window and continued to hyperventilate. Her face was as white as the snow that was sticking to her hair as it fell. "Make that the whole pitcher," Fe shouted, hoping that Jael would hear her down the hallway.

Salima put her hand on Halis' shoulder and pulled her out of the window. Her eyes turned cat like as she looked at Halis. "Everything is going to be okay, little one."

The lines of panic on Halis' face relaxed as Salima and Fe walked her to the bed and sat her down, just as Jael returned with a pitcher and cup.

Two glasses of wine later, the pink returned to Halis' face. She sat on the corner of the bed, shoulders slumped and eyes closed, with one last calming breath she opened her eyes and stood. "I've kept poor Edric waiting long enough."

Halis' eyes lit up as she entered the great hall. Edric sat next to her father on the dais, his leg shaking up and down as he tapped on his knee in rhythm. His breath left him as he stood and gazed at Halis smiling at him from the doorway before she joined him on the dais.

~~~

The summer was over and Halis and Edric were finally settled into their cottage just as the fall winds made their arrival. Rowe sat in his private chamber with Jaren and Kale debating the latest clan meeting. It had been almost a year since he talked to Sarik and still no word on his decision. In the meantime, things were beginning to spiral out of control.

During his visit to Hy-Brasil, Dugun lorded over the clan as if Rowe would never return. Even Kale was ready to put an arrow through him, but Jaren talked him out of it as it might start a war between Canulis and Eir—something Rowe strove to avoid.

"My Laird, the clan can wait no longer. You must select an heir, or they will choose one for you," Kale bellowed, slapping his hand on the table. "And if you leave that oaf in charge again, I will kill him myself," Kale said, gritting his teeth as he fisted his hands.

"And I'm not going to stop him this time," added Jaren sternly pointing to Kale.

"I understand your frustration, but I need more time. If you just give me more time, I promise all will be well and an heir will be chosen," Rowe pleaded.

Letting out a deep calming breath, Kale responded, "You know I believe you, Rowe, but your clan is losing faith in your ability to rule, so I worry."

Rowe sat silently with his hand on his chin as he mentally hashed out a plan. "Kale, is there any way you can convince Tam to court Lenni? I need him to buy me more time."

"You know his heart belongs to Wren. I doubt he would appreciate you playing games with his emotions, Rowe," Kale said with a shrug.

"Lenni refuses to be courted because she keeps having dreams of a man she has never seen and thinks it is her husband to be. My plan is not for them to marry—I know both of their hearts lay elsewhere. I just need to give the clan hope until I get my answer from Sarik," explained Rowe.

"I will talk to him, but I don't like getting the clan's hope up falsely," Kale grumbled.

"I don't like it either, but they leave me little choice. I need more time. I will talk to Lenni. I'm sure she won't mind spending time with Tam as long as she doesn't have to marry him," Rowe reassured Kale. He stood up from his chair, a sign their business was done for the day. "And, Kale, I expect to see Tam over here this evening for supper," he added.

With a slight bow from the doorway Kale replied, "As you wish, my Laird," before departing.

Within the hour Tam arrived at the great hall ready to do his duty to the Laird and the clan. He was greeted by Lenni, who despite her own yearning really did enjoy Tam's company. The two sat by the fire discussing the arrival of Edric's horses earlier that day.

"Tam, you should see the fine horse father has bought for me. She's the most beautiful beast you've ever seen!" exclaimed Lenni as her face lit up against the firelight.

"After Edric teaches you to ride, maybe your father would let me take you on a trip to the cliffs. They're beautiful in the summer, and you could use the fresh air," he offered.

"Oh Tam, that'd be wonderful. I've always wanted to see the cliffs, thank you," she said, leaning over and kissing his cheek.

"Can you believe they're forcing us to spend time with one another like it's a punishment or something?" She laughed, nudging him with her elbow.

"I can't say I'm completely saddened by this mockery as I do enjoy your company. Maybe it'll keep us occupied enough from our own love sorrows that happiness may show upon our brows once again." He smiled and noticed the cook. "Would you like some mead?" he asked before getting up.

"Yes, thank you."

Tam walked across the hall and retrieved two cups of mead. On his way back he noticed his Laird standing in the doorway watching Lenni. Tam looked him in the eyes and smiled before giving him a slight nod of approval. He sat back down beside Lenni and handed her the cup. Tam raised his cup to Lenni and said, "A toast to us. May our courtship be brief but memorable."

"And if not for Dugun, completely nonexistent," she added, before they laughed.

"I should not be laughing at the cause of my broken heart. If not for the fact that my father sent me to Monmalor to deliver salt, I think I would've killed him," Tam confessed as he finished his cup of mead. "Would you like another?" he asked, raising his empty cup.

"I really shouldn't," she replied, before laughing at Tam standing before her with an exaggerated frown. "Very well then, I shall have another." Tam grabbed her cup to refill it.

He returned to the hearth with a pitcher and their two cups in his hand. The two of them sat laughing and drinking mead the rest of the evening. As the fire died down, Tam clasped Lenni's hand in his, bent over, and brought it to his lips. Her face was flushed with drink. She smiled at his gesture and moved closer. A moment later she threw her arms around his neck and kissed his lips. Her kiss stirred something inside of him. Instead of pushing away from her, he pulled her closer, losing himself in her desire and returning her craving with his own until he gently he melted away from her embrace. He leaned his forehead against hers and closed his eyes as he softly caressed her face. "I must go, Lenni," he whispered as he pulled away and walked out the room.

Lenni stood staring after him, her heart beating wildly as her mind swam with confusion. *What in the hell just happened?* she thought, sitting back down in front of the coals that still burned in the hearth. She sat motionless and alone until Jael came looking for her.

Chapter 4

Lenni bolted upright as thunder trailed off in the distance. She grabbed her pounding head and lay back down, rubbing her temples to ease the pain that penetrated her skull. In a single moment of clarity, she became mortified at her actions from last night. Her lips pressed against Tam's betrayed their friendship and left her confused about the lover who haunted her dreams. And yet, excitement grew inside of her just thinking about the taste of mead that hung on his lips as he returned her kiss. He had certainly been a willing participant. Just as Lenni sat up again, Jael walked into the room.

"Well, good morning, sleepy head. Do you plan to sleep the whole day?" Jael smiled.

"I was just getting up, if my head will let me." She blinked a few times then attempted to rub the sleep out of her bloodshot eyes.

"I'd love to know what you did to Tam last night. He has been pacing the great hall like a captured animal all morning. I've never seen him this nervous." Jael raised her brow as she helped Lenni off her bed.

"I don't know what you're talking about, Jael. Nothing happened. We sat by the hearth all night. We drank, we laughed, we kissed and nothing more," she mumbled the last part so Jael would not understand what she said.

Jael laughed. "You kissed Tam?"

Lenni scrunched her face and frowned, causing Jael to laugh so hard, she snorted when she inhaled.

"It's not funny. It was a stupid mistake; I don't know what came over me," she snapped as she attempted to get the knots out of her hair with her fingers. "What a mess. Poor Tam is probably trying to figure out how to get out of this arrangement without making father angry. I don't know what to do." She sighed as she finished braiding her golden blonde hair.

Jael paused for a few seconds before replying. "Tam is an old friend. No matter what you have to say, he'll understand. It's not anger on his face; it's the same confusion that rests upon yours. Just go out there and talk to him. Tell him how you feel," she suggested as she helped Lenni finish dressing.

"That's the problem. I don't know how I feel," Lenni confessed as they walked out of the room.

"And by the look on his face neither does he. I'm sure it's something the two of you can work out together if you talk to one another."

Jael and Lenni walked into the great hall where several people milled about and a few were still eating breakfast. The cook fussed about the kitchen being too hot while Tam mindlessly added more wood to the fire. Tam looked up from the fire, and as soon as he spotted Lenni, he marched over to greet her. Jael squeezed Lenni's hand before leaving her to face Tam alone.

"Morning, my lady, I hope you slept well." Tam bowed to Lenni, but his eyes darted around the room aimlessly. His long awkward pause was a direct contradiction to the confidence he normally projected. He stood straight wringing his hands with a boy-like nervousness.

Lenni sighed and looped her arm in his. "Let's find a more private place to talk," she said somberly, leading him to the private courtyard. Lenni sat on a small bench placed next to the outer wall by Jael several years ago. It was Jael's favorite place to sit and think, and Lenni could see why. Lavender edged the wall leaving its sweet, relaxing scent hanging in the brisk fall air. Tam paced in front of her, his eyes meeting hers every time he turned to walk the other direction.

Tam stopped directly before her and let out a deep breath before finally breaking the silence. "I'm sorry, Lenni. I shouldn't have kissed you, especially while your judgment was clouded. Please forgive me," he pleaded, still keeping his distance as he looked into her eyes.

Lenni reached out, clasped his hand, and pulled him to sit on the bench next to her. "It's I who should apologize, Tam. I'm the one who kissed you, if I recall correctly." Her cheeks blushed from the embarrassment.

"But I didn't stop you as I should have." He pulled his hand away from her and massaged his temples before running his hands through his hair.

"I wish you would have," she lied.

"Do you really?" He cocked his head toward her and scrunched his brow. "Because I don't," he confessed, shaking his head and relaxing his expression. "It reminded me that I'm a man who has needs, ones that can't be ignored forever. My heart breaks for Wren, but I can't pretend I'm unaffected by your kiss, Lenni. Please tell me you felt something too, something more than just remorse." His heart beat faster as he waited for her response.

She looked down, questioning her own emotions before she could contain them no longer. "I feel like I betrayed my heart, Tam. Not because of the kiss, but because of the way I wanted more." She lifted her head to look at him through swollen, tear-filled eyes, emotions painting lines of anguish across her face.

"What do we do, Lenni? Do we deny our yearnings and distance ourselves? Or do we explore these feelings as friends?" Tam wiped away the tears from her face with his thumb, letting his hand gently rest on her cheek.

"How is it not betrayal if you love one and lust after another?" Lenni removed Tam's hand from her cheek.

"I can't betray a love that's not shared, any more than you can. I've waited six years for Wren, and I'm as close to winning her love as you are to winning the heart of this man you have never met. How long do we wait when it's only our hearts that perceive this so called betrayal? No, we should not feel guilty should we find ourselves in each other's arms." A fire sparked in Tam's eyes as he expressed his own convictions.

Tam could see the anguish on Lenni's face and remembered the pain he felt every time his father told him to forget Wren. He did not want to cause Lenni the same pain he detested, so against his better judgment and his heart, he added, "I'm not asking you to give up on the man who haunts your dream. I just want you to give us a chance." He placed his hand on hers.

She pulled her hand away. "And what if one of us falls in love with the other? What then?" She looked off into the distance.

It was too late. He had already fallen in love with her and would say anything not to scare her away. Hands in his pockets, he fumbled around with a gift he brought for Lenni, but he removed his hands without the present and shrugged. "I don't have all the answers, Lenni, but I know no matter what, you and I will always be friends."

Lenni stood and faced him. "I'm afraid you could be mistaken. If we were both free, you'd be the one I'd choose to give my heart to, but we're not. And I'm done with this nonsense father has put us up to. If we continue this charade, we're both going to end up hurt, and that's something I'm not willing to take part in."

Tam stood to meet her gaze. "Lenni, I hope that when you find out where your heart belongs, it won't be too late." He turned and walked away.

Tears streamed down her face as she watched him leave more confused than she had been before. How could something as simple as a kiss between friends cause so much pain? Now that he was gone, her heart ached for him. Already she regretted her decision; their kiss would haunt her forever. Finding the man who invaded her dreams was the only way to know for certain where her heart lay.

〜〜〜

The long overdue message finally arrived from Sarik. Rowe sat behind the table in his private chamber mulling over each and every word. It was written in the language of Sarik's people, something Rowe learned from Sarik many years ago. Unlike the other messages sent by Sarik on parchment, this one was on stark white paper brighter than anything Rowe had seen, and each letter of each word was precisely the same size and unusually perfect. It was more than just a simple missive, and Salima's help was required to understand its contents. He walked into the hallway, looking for someone who could retrieve Salima. Tam hurried down the hall past him without even acknowledging his laird when Rowe called for him to a halt.

"My boy, where are you going in such a rush?" Rowe asked, but didn't wait for a reply. "No matter. I need for you to ride to Halis and Edric's cottage. Tell Salima I have received a message from Sarik and require her assistance."

"Yes, my Laird," was all he said as he rushed out of the house. He padded his way to the stable, mounted his stag pony and headed to Halis and Edric's house. In his haste, he dropped in the stable a small pouch containing a polished stone wrapped in silver on a leather necklace. He intended to give it to Lenni, but their conversation took them to a different place, and now his token was a reminder of yet another failed attempt at love.

He rode down the well-trodden road, his mind in turmoil over Lenni's rejection. Just as he approached the cottage, the sound of laughter singing from the windows caused Tam to stop and listen for a moment. He sighed and blotted his eyes with the edge of his sleeve, amazed that something as simple as a woman in love's laughter could bring him to tears. *How is it that something so unassuming continues to elude me?* he thought before knocking on the door. Halis answered, threw her arms around Tam's neck, and kissed his cheek.

"Tam, I've missed you, dear brother. Come in," she bubbled, happy as always.

"I can't stay long. I'm here to deliver a message to Salima from your father," he said, craning his head around the cottage looking for her. Edric shook Tam's hand as he stepped inside the doorway.

"She's out back collecting plants." Halis grinned as she grabbed Tam's hand and lead him out the backdoor where Salima was bent over in the garden.

Salima stood and turned her gaze toward them. "Tam, what brings you here?"

"Rowe has received word from Hy-Brasil and requires your help," he relayed.

She picked up the basket by her feet and followed them back into the cottage.

"Did he tell you what it was concerning?" she asked, carefully wrapping the contents of the basket in a cloth.

"No, but it must be quite urgent if he had me ride out here to get you."

"Aw...Can't you stay and visit?" protested Halis.

"I can ride back on my own, Tam, if you would like to stay," said Salima.

"I could use your help. I need to add thatch to the roof and could use someone tall enough to hand it to me. Not to mention, a break from all of Halis' jabbering," Edric teased.

"I suppose I could stay," Tam relented, as Halis smiled and threw her arms around him again.

As soon as Salima left, Tam followed Edric out back where the thatch was already bundled. He climbed onto the roof and waited for Tam to hand him a bundle. Tam looked off in the distance lost in thought. Edric cleared his voice from edge of the roof, snapping Tam back to reality. "Want to talk about it?"

"What makes you think I have something to talk about?" Tam asked as he handed Edric a bundle of thatch, attempting to hide his nervousness.

"Did you really think your kiss with Lenni would go unnoticed? The prospect of a union between you and Lenni has tongues wagging from here to Monmalor," Edric said, grabbing the bundle from Tam.

Throwing his hands up in the air, Tam groaned. "What a fine mess that kiss turned out to be. I always believed in my undying love for Wren, but after that kiss—I don't know. I yearn for Lenni in a way I never felt for Wren. And after toiling all night over it, I came to the conclusion the Wren of the past is dead, and it's time I move on. Unfortunately, Lenni does not share my willingness to let go of the past. She still believes she will find this man from her dreams."

"A great man once told me, think hard before you set your sights on one of Rowe's daughters. They're nothing but torment to any man who opens his heart to them—but a fine torment, indeed." He laughed.

"Well, that man is more fool than great at the moment," snorted Tam.

"But you can't deny you were wrong either," said Edric as he placed the last bundle on the roof and climbed down.

~~~

Salima sat across the table from Rowe and translated Sarik's letter to him.

Dear Rowe, Laird of Eir,

My apologies for not responding sooner, but I have my reasons for the delay. I was selfish when I did not give you an immediate response upon your last visit. Thirty years is inconsequential to me as you so intrepidly pointed out, so I would be honored to spend it in the service of a friend. I will agree to marry your daughter, but only under these conditions—

Salima looked up from her translation to add her own thoughts. "I'm shocked he has agreed. I will read each condition and explain it to you. If you disagree, we will need to address that in the reply."

Jael is to be given the right to refuse. I will not have her against her will.

"I would not want to force her either, so we agree on this point," said Rowe.

We shall reside in Hy-Brasil for the first year and then we will alternate every six months between Hy-Brasil and Eir. I will hire carpenters to build us a residence in a location of your choosing.

"Might I suggest the cliffs in the northern coast? Knowing Sarik, he will want to build a fortress of stone unlike any you have seen. This area will provide a good location for protection should the clan need it," reasoned Salima.

"That would be a good location, but I fear it might be too difficult to build on," explained Rowe.

"It will not be a problem for Sarik," she replied.

Jael is to keep all particulars of Hy-Brasil secret as you have, or she will have to spend the remainder of her days exiled there.

"She will have to sign the same contract you did on your first trip to Hy-Brasil," she reminded him.

It is up to me whether Jael and I have children together. If I decline to carry out this duty, she will be allowed to choose whomever she feels fit to perform this task in my absence—but only if I decline this function.

"This is Sarik's way of saying he feels no need to provide an heir if the marriage is only one of mutual convenience, but leaves her room to provide an heir for her clan," she explained.

"I am not in favor of this. It would be wrong for her to have children by someone other than her husband," he objected.

"You must remember, Rowe. Sarik is only agreeing to this union for the protection of your clan. Which reminds me, is he aware of Jael's unique birth?"

"No. And I intend to keep it that way," Rowe responded bluntly.

"I don't know if that is a good idea. It might be a major deal breaker if he finds out she might out live him," she replied.

"Good idea or not, I can't afford for him to back out."

Salima sat silently for a few seconds before continuing.

All said children are to be born in Hy-Brasil. It is up to King Varen whether or not any of these children will be included in Hy-Brasil's line of succession.

"Assuming she has children, they are all to be born in our hospital, for her safety as well as the child's. There is no guarantee any will rule Hy-Brasil. I doubt King Varen is happy with this arrangement, as temporary as it is intended to be, so he is most likely treating it like a contract of protection rather than a union of people."

"Knowing King Varen's people as I do, I can understand his disapproval of the situation. I understand even if Sarik and Jael have children together those children will have no claim to Hy-Brasil," Rowe assured her.

The rules and laws of Hy-Brasil are to hold dominion over those of Eir.

"Honestly, I don't know why he has added this to the contract. You will have to ask him, yourself," she said.

Neither shall rule the other's realm except jointly. Upon the untimely death of either party, the rule shall revert to those listed in each perspective realm's written line of succession.

"This is to protect the rule of Hy-Brasil in the event Sarik should die. It ensures the line of succession regardless of Jael's claim as wife. In return, it also ensures all claims to Eir will remain within your clan—Sarik has no intention of ruling without Jael," she stated.

Kale's son Tam is to be named my primary council in Eir.

"He needs no contract for this. Tam will make a wonderful council. I have been teaching him to run the clan since he was a boy so I could make him Laird. Not that things worked out that way," he pointed out.

"I figured you would have no problem with that." She laughed.

As far as the delay, our laws prevent me from making contracts with minors. We must wait until Jael has reached the age of eighteen before we can pursue this matter any further. I will expect her to be sent to Hy-Brasil after her birthday. She will have one lunar cycle to accept or decline this contract. At which point, I will either send her home alone or accompany her back to Eir so we may wed according to your customs and in front of her clan as validation of the marriage.

His Royal Highness,
Prince Sarik Alexander Poseidon of Hy-Brasil

"I want to wait until after Jael's birthday to tell her—I don't want to give her too much time to over think the situation." He leaned back in his chair and rubbed the side of his face. "I would like for you to accompany her, Salima. She respects your opinion and will need someone she can rely on to be truthful."

"I don't agree with keeping her uniqueness a secret from Jael or Sarik. I know Sarik, and it won't take long for him to figure out what she is. I understand we are all sworn to secrecy, even King Varen himself keeps quiet, but they should know," Salima urged, hoping to change his mind.

"I can't afford to tell them until after they are wed," he said. "I promise, if they make it through their first year of marriage, I will tell them both. Please don't say anything."

"Very well, Rowe. You have until their first anniversary; after that, I will do it myself," she warned, shaking her finger at him.

"Fair enough." He sighed before standing and opening the door for Salima to leave. "Oh, I forgot to ask. How does Halis like her new cottage?"

"She is thankful you did not build it next to the stables. She says it is enough that Edric brings home the smell every day."

"Could you find Lenni and Tam for me please? I want to let them know they only have to keep up their courtship until Jael's birthday.

~~~

Night fell and still no one could find Lenni. Her horse was missing from the stable, so Rowe sent out everyone he could find to look for her, fearful she might have fallen and hurt herself. It was not like Lenni to leave and not let anyone know where she was going. One by one the searchers returned empty handed until there was none left searching, save Tam. Darkness encompassed the forest making it too dangerous to go back out. They would have to wait until morning to start their search again.

Tam sat on his stag pony, loosely holding its ropes. The pony followed the well-cut trail to Monmalor—a trail it knew even in the dark. "It's all my fault, Farth," he said to the pony patting its neck. "I'm the reason she ran away. I should've left well enough alone, but no! I had to tell her of my lust as if she were a common wench. Is it any wonder I keep scaring them away?"

Farth whinnied as if to agree.

"I should've told her how I really felt. How she makes my heart race every time I see her. Her touch burns my skin like fire, unlike any woman I have known—not even Wren could

stir in me what Lenni does," he confessed as the pony
continued along the trail.

Soon Farth could no longer find his way and Tam was
forced to camp for the night. Come morning he would search
for the prints he followed from the stable, the ones made by
her horse. With her inexperience on horseback, Tam hoped to
find her before nightfall. He pulled his bag off his horse and
searched for seasoned wood to build a fire. Although it was
early fall, a nip settled in the air leaving him chilled.

He arranged his blanket and stretched his legs so the fire
could warm his unbooted feet. He pulled out a small, fabric-
wrapped parcel containing bread and dried meats. Carefully
he unwrapped his meal and began to eat. After a couple of
bites, he washed it down with water from his goatskin
container. He sat for a few minutes and inhaled deeply, then
yelled into the darkness, "Lenni...I love you!" before lying
down for the night.

In the darkness Lenni heard the sound of someone calling
her name. She was cold and hungry; every muscle in her body
ached, and she was alone. In the distance, she saw a small
fire, so she grabbed the rope to her horse and walked closer
until she reached the shadows thrown by the fire. She let go
of the horse and quietly crept behind the trees until she was
close enough to see Tam by the fire. She let out a sigh and
rushed to where he lay.

Tam jumped to his feet at the noise, and Lenni threw arms
around him.

"You scared the life out of me!" he exclaimed, wrapping
his arms around her. "Why did you run away? Your father is
consumed with worry," he reprimanded.

She looked up with tear-filled eyes. "I'm sorry," she cried,
her voice raspy from the ride.

"So am I, Lenni. What did I do to make you want to leave in such haste?" he asked as he sat down on the blanket and motioned for her to sit next to him.

She leaned into his warm arms. "It's not you, Tam. The problem is me," she paused. "I'm in love with two people, one who is a ghost and one who is very much real." She gazed at him and smiled.

She shivered, so Tam pulled her closer to his chest and rubbed her goose-bumped arms. "Are you hungry?" he asked, hearing her stomach grumble.

"I'm starving," she replied.

He reached into his bag and handed her some bread and meat.

Taking a bite of the bread and swallowing, she smiled. "I don't know how to thank you. I shouldn't have left without leaving word, but until I find him, I'll never know where my heart belongs."

"Then I'll help you find him," said Tam against his better judgment. He stood and wrapped her in his blanket, then walked into the forest to find more wood for the fire.

Lenni was too tired to question Tam's motives. She finished the last of his food and sat shivering next to the dying fire. A few minutes later, Tam returned from the forest with an arm full of wood. He carefully stacked the wood on the coals then settled next to her.

Once Lenni warmed, she curled up next to Tam and slept.

Chapter 5

The sun came up over the hills as Lenni opened her eyes. Tam's arm and leg draped across her body wrapping Lenni in a cocoon of warmth—a stark contrast to the cold morning air. She shifted to wrench herself out from under him, but he pulled her closer and whispered, "Don't leave me." His breath burned against her neck. She closed her eyes and mentally tried to push back the desire that built inside of her.

"Tam, we need to get started if we plan to make it to Monmalor before nightfall."

He inhaled the sweet scent of her hair, then opened his eyes and smiled. Her face, only inches from his, was too tempting not to touch. He lightly kissed her cheek before unwrapping his arms and legs. Standing, he stretched his long, well-formed body, which did not go unnoticed by Lenni, then helped her up from the blanket.

"There's a small town half way to Monmalor where we can find food and provisions. Did you bring coins with you?" he asked as he folded the blanket and laid it across his pony's back.

"I have some, but not much. Um...Is there a place—"

"Behind those bushes is a fallen log and a little privacy," he broke in, pointing to a small cluster of bushes not far from where the animals grazed.

"Thank you," she said as she made her way there.

Tying his bow and bag to Lenni's horse, Tam waited for her.

Lenni emerged; she walked up to Farth and petted him on the head. "Tam, would you mind if I rode Farth? I'm uncomfortable riding Freya—she's too hard for me to mount."

Raising his eyebrows, Tam chuckled. "You named her after the goddess of love?"

"Yes, that way she might bring me luck when it comes to finding my own love."

"Freya, I believe we are destined to become close friends," he said, patting the horse's neck. Farth whinnied, and Tam laughed. "I don't believe Farth is very fond of the idea," he mused then grabbed Lenni by the waist and lifted her onto Farth's back.

By noon they reached a small village where they could eat and rest. Tam found a merchant who was on his way to Halor and sent a message to Rowe that they were well and headed to Monmalor. Within the hour they resumed their journey and were back in the forest.

A few miles down the road, Lenni stopped Farth and directed her attention to Tam. "Why are you helping me find another man?"

Tam turned Freya around and faced Lenni. He thought for a second then looked up and took a deep breath before meeting her gaze. "The sooner we find him, the sooner I can move on with my life; plus, there's no way I'd let you go about the country alone and unprotected. Your father would have my head if anything happened to you."

"I'm glad to have your company, even if it confuses my heart. If I don't find him within the year, I'll give up searching," she promised.

After spending the rest of the day in relative silence, they made it to Harwell, Monmalor's largest township, just as darkness began to fall. Lenni cringed with every step Farth took. This was the longest trip she had ever made and her body reminded her of it. Stopping at the inn's stables, Tam dismounted Freya then put his hands around Lenni's waist to help her down. The instant her feet touched the ground, she threw her arms around his neck as her knees buckled. Tam wrapped his arm around her tightly and pulled her against his broad chest to steady her. Once she could stand, she released her grip and allowed her hands to slide down to his chest, her fingers soaking in the heat emanating off of it. Her exhausted body craved his touch and refused to push away despite the disapproval of the voice in her head.

Tam let go of his embrace. "Are you okay?"

"I'm fine. I didn't realize spending all day on a pony would turn my legs to jelly."

He looped his arm around her waist and helped her to the inn. After paying for the room, he brought in his belongings and put them on the floor near the hearth. The room was small but clean; one single pallet lay on the floor with a stool next to it. Lenni stopped in the doorway with a priggish expression. "Tam, I must insist we have separate rooms," she commanded, refusing to enter farther.

"My lady Lenni, you forget the size of your coin purse. If you expect us to have a roof over our heads and food in our bellies the next few days, we'll have to share," he responded motioning to the tiny room.

"Very well, but I'm not comfortable with the situation at all," she huffed, putting her hands on her hips.

Tam ignored her and unpacked a clean shirt and pants from his bag. "The keeper said there's a river nearby if you wish to bathe; otherwise, he'll have someone bring a bucket of water to clean ourselves. Personally, I feel like I am wearing the road and would prefer a bath and clean clothes."

"I'm a complete idiot. I brought nothing with me," she told him.

"I noticed your lack of provisions this morning when I readied the animals. Lucky for you I know the innkeeper. His daughter is about your size and has offered you use of one of her shifts, so that your clothes can be washed," explained Tam.

"I can't walk back from the river in just a shift, nor do I care to leave myself so bare in your presence, particularly in bed," she protested.

"Lenni, you have nothing to worry about, least of all your maidenhood. A clean shift is all you have, so it will have to do. You can always wrap yourself in a blanket on the way back from the river, but we need to go now before it gets cold," Tam argued as a knock sounded on the door.

It was the innkeeper's daughter with a clean shift, a towel, and a sliver of lavender scented soap. "For your lady wife," she said, curtsied and handed the items to Tam.

Tam shut the door and turned around to see Lenni's face completely red.

"Why did you tell them I'm your wife," she snapped and pursed her lips.

"I didn't want to damage your reputation. Many here know your father, word would spread like wildfire if they thought you were here with a man who's not your husband," he explained. "Now let's go to the river."

*** ～～ ***

Lenni was missing for two days before Rowe got the message from Tam. He let out a sigh of relief that she was safe. He was not happy about their decision to go on a quest.

The only consolation was Tam would be with her. Unfortunately, Kale was livid at his son for not returning home and just as angry at Rowe for allowing it to happen.

"This is your fault!" he exclaimed, pacing the inside of Rowe's private chamber. "First, you break that boy's heart by allowing Wren to marry Dugun, even though you trained him to be Laird. Now Lenni is stringing him along while she looks for another man. Then when you finally decided to betroth Jael, you do so to Sarik. What has Tam ever done to you to deserve such treatment?" Kale's voice was laced with anger as he fisted his hands and continued to pacing the floor in front of the hearth.

"Tam is like a son, Kale, and I'm sure he has reasons for following Lenni instead of bringing her home. I chose Sarik for Jael because my problem is Dugun, and even Tam would have trouble besting him. He builds an army near the border at Annoc, and you know as well as I do, Tam wouldn't have a chance if you or I weren't here."

Kale put his hand above the hearth and leaned against it facing the fire. He watched the flames dance in front of him as Rowe's words sunk in. "I know he's no match for Dugun physically and has little experience with an army, but he's more than capable of running this clan," Kale stated, looking back to Rowe.

"A fact I am well aware of, and the reason Sarik has chosen him as council. I understand how Sarik thinks. He needs Tam to keep this clan together, so when it comes to the day to day business, it will be Tam's job to run the clan," Rowe explained. "I have not given up hope that Lenni will come to her senses and marry him—and apparently neither has Tam. I don't believe he would concede to her wishes if he had," Rowe added, watching Kale's anger melt from his face.

Kale sighed and sat in the chair across from Rowe. "I hope she doesn't break his heart. He's a good man and deserves to find love."

"According to Tam's message they need provisions and coin. Neither of them planned for this trip, so Tam only has a small pack and no coin, and Lenni left with enough money for a couple days, if she is thrifty, but that is all. I'll have Jael make a pack for her. Do you think Ugis would want to help Edric bring a couple horses back to Monmalor and deliver the pack?" Rowe asked.

"Work has slowed at the mill, so I'm sure he wouldn't mind going with Edric," replied Kale.

"I'll talk to him tonight. If I know Tam, he'll wait in Harwell at the inn on the edge of town until he has gotten word from me. As long as he's in Monmalor, he might as well work on the trade route we discussed last year and see how well the extra security at the southern border is working. It'll save me from having to go out there myself." Rowe pulled a parchment and small stick of charcoaled willow vine from his desk. "I'll send word for them to return before Jael's marriage during the winter solstice. I'm sure Sarik will want to talk to him before returning to Hy-Brasil."

"When are you planning to tell Jael about this arrangement? The solstice is less than two months away."

"I am telling her today. The longboat is preparing to leave by week's end."

"The waters are treacherous this time of year. Why does Sarik not send a sky ship?" Kale asked.

"He's trying to keep everything secret until she is there. The longboat and crew are from Hy-Brasil. They are masters at predicting the sea and weather and can make the trip in less than a half a day," stated Rowe.

Kale stood up to leave. "I must talk to Ugis if you expect him to leave tomorrow," he said as he walked towards the door.

"I'll see you tomorrow morn. We still have business to discuss," said Rowe, as he opened the door for Kale.

~~

Jael sat on the bench in the courtyard, like she had done a thousand times. Her mind was still reeling from the conversation she had with her father, and although she did not wish to remain a maiden her whole life, the man her father chose was a far cry from what she wished for in a husband. The thought of being married to a man more than thirty years her senior made her stomach lurch. Why had her father chosen her for this task? She had an older, unmarried sister and always believed herself to be the favorite. Her father's betrayal stung her eyes.

She played back his words in her mind. "I know this is not what you had planned, but things have changed. We need a strong heir for the clan, and Prince Sarik is doing this out of friendship. I know you have never met him, and despite your age difference, he would make a good husband and strong ally," her father explained.

"I'm to be married to an old man for the sake of Eir?" Jael had never known her father to waver from his belief that his daughters should marry for love, so his sudden change of heart confused her.

He paced the floor in front of the hearth in his private chambers. "I made this decision with a heavy heart. I can no longer wait on your sisters to give me a grandson, nor can I trust any of their husbands. I need Sarik to help rule when I am gone and can think of no better daughter to rule with him."

Tears fell down her face. "But he is so old!" Jael cried, hoping he would change his mind at the sight of her tears.

Rowe sat in his chair and put his fingertips together under his chin. "I have arranged for you to leave for Hy-Brasil at week's end. You will stay there a full lunar cycle, and if you still feel you are unable to wed him by the end of the time, you may come home, and I will offer him Lenni."

She stifled her tears as his word sunk in. She would be given a chance to turn the marriage down. "If that is your wish, my Laird, I will do my best to honor it." Jael curtsied and left the room.

Night fell while she sat on the bench, and Jael shivered as the cold wind started to blow. The sound of horses at the front of the house caught her attention, so she went to investigate. Halis and Edric had just arrived from their cottage. Jael rushed to her sister and threw her arms around her as if she hadn't seen her in years.

As soon as Halis saw Jael's tearstained face, she frowned and said to Edric, "I'll see you in the great room later," before walking off with Jael.

"What troubles you, sister?" she asked as they walked to the room she and Jael had shared.

"Father has betrothed me to Prince Sarik," she cried.

Halis stopped dead in her tracks. She looked at Jael for a second then cocked her head to the side. "Please tell me you're joking. Prince Sarik is older than father, and what of his promise to allow us to marry for love?"

"Apparently, Dugun is such a threat father feels this is the only way to protect the clan," she said as she dried her eyes with her sleeve.

"That's awful, Jael. When will this take place?" asked Halis.

"I leave for Hy-Brasil in six days. I have one lunar cycle to make my decision." Jael sighed.

"You leave on your birthday? I'm so glad I'm not father's favorite." She laughed.

Jael chuckled as they started to walk again. They strolled into the frigid room they once shared. Jael looked at the hearth stacked with wood and motioned her hand towards the pile— within seconds the fire started.

"I wonder what Prince Sarik will say when he finds out you can do that," said Halis as she made herself comfortable on the pallet.

Jael sat down beside Halis and sighed, "Well, I wonder what he is going to say when he finds out I can do this." Jael kneeled on the floor then stretched out her arms in front of her as her body began to grow hair and shrink until she was entirely hidden beneath her clothes. The clothes moved around, making Halis scoot back on the pallet in fear before a small cat emerged from the fabric's folds.

Halis laughed as she picked up the cat. She held it under its front leg at arm's length and looked into its eyes. "He will most likely die of shock," she laughed, putting Jael back down on the floor. Jael rubbed against Halis and purred loudly before she jumped on the bed and curled up next to her. Halis looked down at the little white cat and said, "On the bright side, if he dies of shock you'll no longer have to worry about being married to him."

A minute later, Jael turned back to her human form. "I doubt he'll find it as amusing as you do," she said as she dressed.

"When did you learn to shape shift?"

"A couple of months ago I was watching the swallows fly outside the window and began to daydream about flying. Next thing I knew, I sprouted feathers—it scared me half to death, but it didn't take me long to figure out it was something I could control."

"You should be happy, you will finally get your chance to go to Hy-Brasil," remarked Halis.

"Under these conditions, I'd rather not go at all," groaned Jael.

"I'm not ready to get married, Halis. I don't even know what it's like to kiss a man, let alone perform wifely duties. I want to know what it's like to love and be loved in return." Jael sighed, sitting down next to Halis.

Putting her arm around Jael, Halis hugged her.

~~~

A week passed and Jael was on a large ship headed to Hy-Brasil to meet her future husband. She was nervous about the meeting, and after many talks with her father, she knew regardless of her feelings for Sarik she would marry him for the clan.

Once the ship left dock, Salima told Jael her image was not her true form. Before Jael's eyes, Salima changed. Her skin turned blue as the sky and her eyes looked more cat-like than human. Instead of the shock Salima expected, Jael asked if she could conjure fire. In a single motion, a ball of fire appeared in Salima's hand. She moved it back and forth between her fingers before out stretching her arm over the side of the boat and allowing the fire to roll into the water. Jael's eyes widened in amazement.

The ship moved swiftly across the sea. Its black sails shimmered with tiny strands of gold woven throughout the oddly slick fabric. When Jael inquired, she was told it was a solar sail, and although Salima explained how it worked, most of what she said was as foreign as Hy-Brasil itself.

As the boat approached the island, Jael looked out over the rail taking in the magnificence. The city was beautiful and unlike any she had ever seen. It was made of concentric rings of land that surrounded the harbor. Plants, flowers, and trees covered every inch, including many of the houses, and in the center of the rings sat a massive city of metal and glass that was beautiful beyond belief. Moments later the ship laid anchor in the harbor of Atlantis, the capital city of Hy-Brasil.

A delegation from King Varen was waiting for them at the dock. Most of the people were older men, advisers to the King, but one stood out among them. He couldn't have been more than five years older than Jael. He was tall with raven hair and eyes bluer than the sea. He was the most handsome creature Jael ever set eyes on. He noticed her stare and smiled. Jael lowered her eyes and blushed. It was unladylike to look at a man that way, especially while on her way to meet her future husband… but, the gods be damned, this man had gotten to her already.

He walked over, kneeled down, and kissed her hand.

"Welcome to Hy-Brasil, Lady Jael. I hope you will decide stay with us."

His eyes looked into hers and Jael lost herself in them. Her heart raced as a shiver went down her spine. Jael had to remember her place. She pulled her hand away reluctantly. If she would be future queen, this type of behavior was not acceptable. She addressed the man in front of her. "Where I come from it is treason to be so bold to a lady betrothed, especially one betrothed to one's prince," she retorted, almost ashamed of his behavior, and yet, she could not forget the feeling of his touch.

"Then I should introduce myself." Standing up inches from her face, he said, "I'm Prince Sarik. Sorry to have startled you, my lady." He nodded his head in a slight bow.

How could he possibly be the prince? Jael's father had known Prince Sarik his whole life, and even then, Sarik was considered the elder of the two. "My apologies, your highness, I assumed you'd appear longer in years. Forgive me." She stepped back and curtsied low to the ground.

He clutched her hands pulling Jael to her feet. "There are few who know of our secrets, and your father is one of them. I believe we have much to talk about, Lady Jael." Sarik offered Jael his arm and walked her to a covered seated area he called a transport vehicle.

Chapter 6

Tam swung open the door to their room and announced from the doorway, "Look what I found wandering around town today."

As Tam stepped inside the room, Ugis peeped his head around the doorframe and said, "Hello, Lenni."

She jumped up from the stool and threw her arms around his neck squealing, "Ugis!" then she noticed Halis' husband Edric next to him in the hallway and squealed again, "Edric!" When she looked down, she realized they were carrying her trunk from home. "My clothes!" she exclaimed, throwing her arms around the trunk. "I have missed you so much and vow never to leave you again as long as I live."

"Again she breaks my heart as she confesses her true love to another." Tam laughed while Edric and Ugis hauled the trunk into the small room.

Ugis reached into his travel bag and pulled out a pouch of coins. "This is for you. Rowe wanted to make sure his daughter didn't have to spend one more day at that god forsaken inn, as he put it," Ugis relayed to Tam.

Tam laughed. "At least there's enough coin for Lenni to have a hot bath. She drove me crazy with her constant complaints about the cold river."

Lenni tilted her head and stuck her tongue out at Tam before asking, "What news do you have from home?"

"Your father betrothed your sister to Prince Sarik, and you are both expected to be at the wedding during the solstice," Ugis announced, handing Tam the parchment from Rowe.

Tam and Lenni were speechless, utterly shocked by what Ugis said. "My father did what?" Lenni exclaimed, before turning her attention to Tam. "Is that why father wanted you to pretend to court me? He was waiting on a betrothal offer from Prince Sarik?" She glared at Tam and fisted her hands to her side.

"If it was, I had no idea. Your father just said he needed more time, and he never told me why."

Edric cleared his voice from the doorway. "I think we should carry this conversation to the great room. I'm starving and there's not enough room for all of us in this broom closet."

"That's the best suggestion I've heard all week besides." He laughed from the doorway. "You coming, Lenni?"

Lenni opened the trunk and riffled through her clothes. "You go ahead. I'll meet you after I've changed...two or three times," she said, mumbling the last part of her sentence.

"I understand you wish to spend time with your true love in private. I shall leave you two alone," Tam dramatized, and Lenni rolled her eyes and laughed.

The men sat one of the benched tables that littered the room. The fire was warm and the smell of stew filled the air as the innkeeper's daughter served dinner from the pot that hung over the fireplace. She placed the wooden bowls in front of each of the men just as Lenni walked into the room. Lenni's golden hair had been brushed, braided, and tied up so the nape of her neck showed, and her sky blue dress perfectly matched the color of her eyes. Tam stared as she walked over and sat next to him.

"Umm, that smells wonderful," she gushed, her stomach rumbling.

Tam could smell the faint waft of lavender that clung to her skin and whispered in her ear, "So do you."

Her cheeks blushed as she nudged him away with her elbow. "It feels good to be clean and to have my clothes."

"Edric thinks we should check the western port at Blackrock next. He says there has been a lot of traffic there with Beakers bringing pottery," said Tam, before taking a bite of his stew.

"I wonder if they have new fabrics. I'd like a new dress for Jael's wedding," Lenni commented.

"They've opened a fabric shop near the docks next to the fish market. Do you think Halis would like a new dress too?" Edric asked.

"What a silly question. What woman wouldn't like a new dress?" pointed out Lenni.

"If I give you coin, can you get her one too?"

"Is there a certain color or cut you would like?"

"You're her sister and know her better than I do. I'm sure she would be happy with anything you pick out," he said.

"Yes, but she would cherish it forever if she knew you picked it out for her," Lenni explained, attempting to educate Edric.

"I didn't think she'd care," he replied.

"Well, you're mistaken. You see, we ladies like to feel our man is thinking of us, even if it's as simple as picking a dress color," she clarified.

He thought for a moment. "Then could you please pick her out something in green? I'd love to see her fiery red hair against a dark green background," he conveyed with a smile as he pictured it.

"I think we should leave tomorrow, Tam. I'm tired of Harwell and this quaint little hellhole you refer to as an inn," complained Lenni.

"Edric, where are you and Ugis headed?" asked Tam.

"We're headed to my father's to pick up a couple of horses he promised me once the stable was built. His home is on the other side of Monmalor, a full day's ride. We will head out in the morning. You and Lenni should ride with us. Dunfin is only a half-day's ride to Blackrock and would be a good place to stop at for the night," Edric suggested.

"I think we might take you up on your offer. It's safer for us to travel in a group, plus we'll need your stag pony for Lenni's trunk. Are you sure your parents won't mind?" Tam asked.

"Not at all. My mother will enjoy the company. According to father, she has a hard time adjusting to not having any children to care for. My poor father does not appreciate the attention she has focused on him." Edric laughed.

"I wish I had your problem, Edric. Our mother wishes we would settle down, move out, and give her grandchildren. At least Ugis has found interest in Jaren's daughter, so she's hopeful." Tam grinned, then finished the remainder of his stew.

~~~

The faintest hint of morning began to light the woods. Tam rode close to Lenni for the first couple of hours. She kept falling asleep, and he was afraid she would fall off and hurt herself. When they finally stopped to rest and eat, Ugis tossed a cup of cold water in her face.

Lenni gasped in shock as the cold liquid hit her. "What did you do that for?" she squealed, wiping her face with the cloth Ugis handed her.

"It's for your own safety, Lenni. You need to wake up before you fall off of Farth, and if you keep us at this pace, it'll take us a week to get to Dunfin," Ugis replied before sitting on a rock and eating his breakfast.

Tam scowled at Ugis.

"What? I know you were thinking the same thing," he said to Tam.

Walking over to Lenni, Tam helped her get the last of the water off her face then apologized. "I'm sorry my brother lacks the manners his mother taught him. Are you okay?"

"I'm awake if that's what you mean by okay," she said, looking daggers at Ugis.

"My apologies, Lenni. I should not have treated a lady so curtly, please forgive me," Ugis apologized.

"I should've expected nothing less from a little brother," she jeered, tying the wet tendrils from around her face into a knot at the top of her head.

A few minutes later, they were back on the trail. The rest of the ride to Dunfin was uneventful and went much quicker.

Night was already upon them by the time they arrived at Edric's father's home. His vast estate was the largest in Monmalor; horse and sheep pastures lined each side of the road until they reached the great wooden home at the end. Laird Dunfin welcomed them in the courtyard that sat to the front of the house. He was much older than Rowe and looked worse for the wear, but he was overjoyed to see Edric, the youngest of his children and the last to leave home.

The accommodations were far better than they had been at the inn, so Lenni was willing to spend a few more days there at the insistence of the Lady Dunfin, who spent a considerable amount of time coddling a much embarrassed Edric and entertaining Lenni. By week's end, Tam knew they needed to move on despite Lenni's contented state and complete unwillingness to go anywhere. There was only one lunar cycle left until they had to return to Eir and set Lenni's man-hunt aside, and Tam still to check on the port for Rowe.

"Lenni, stop dawdling. We need to leave," shouted Tam from the back of Freya.

"Must I leave my trunk behind?" She frowned as she hung her bag over Farth's back.

"Unless you plan on carrying it in your lap, yes. I promise we will stop back here on our way home. Ugis and Edric will wait for our return to Dunfin before we all head home together," said Tam.

"Can't we use a pack animal?" she pleaded as Edric helped her onto Farth's back.

"There have been problems with brigands lately, and I don't want to be burdened with pack animals. If you do not wish to be parted from your comfortable bed and pretty dresses, you can stay here and forget your search," Tam offered, attempting to sway her from continuing her quest.

Lenni sighed and said nothing further as they began their trip to Blackrock. Traveling along the well-formed trail Laird Dunfin advised them to take, the sun warmed the chilled air as it climbed high in the sky. Lenni closed her eyes as she rode. It had been awhile since they last stopped, but they were almost there, and Tam didn't want to lose any more time. A vision began to form in her mind much like the one of her mystery man. This time there were arrows flying in front of her, the whistle of their fletching penetrated her ears. As she looked to Tam an arrow impaled his chest and knocking him to the ground. Lenni gasped and opened her eyes, her heart beating out of control as she saw Tam still mounted on Freya and looking at her like she was possessed by demons. "We need to get off this trail," she gasped, still recovering from her vision.

"What is going on, Lenni?" Worry crossed his brow.

"Just do as I ask," she snapped, panic welled up inside of her.

"Very well, but be warned, I don't know my way around here. We could end up lost," he replied, turning his horse off the main path and onto a small side trail.

Lenni let out a deep breath before whispering to herself, "I would rather you be lost than dead."

Minutes after they left the trail, an arrow crossed just in front of Tam's face. He yelled for Lenni to hold on before kicking Farth in the haunch. They rode hard until they could see the edge of the forest, and once Tam felt they were safe, they slowed to a canter and then a walk. He could tell by the look on Lenni's face now was not the time to question what just happened.

They quickly rode to the inn Laird Dunfin suggested and checked in. Tam opened the door to their room; unlike the inn in Harwell this room was large and inviting. A bedraggled Lenni stood in the room almost disappointed at the fact there were two beds instead of one. She sat in one of the two chairs next to a small table.

Tam shut the door behind him with his foot and threw their bags on the floor. He sat in the chair opposite Lenni, leaned his elbow on the table and massages his temples with his fingers. "What in the hell happened out there?" he calmly asked, dropping his hand to look at her.

Before she could reply, she wailed hysterically, tears streaming down her face as she stared at the blank wall across from her. Tam got up from his seat, knelt and wrapped his arms around her. After a moment he let go and wiped the tears from her face with his thumbs. Looking into his green eyes, she calmed herself long enough to speak.

"I saw...*sniff*...I saw a vision and ...*sniff.* There were arrows everywhere," she cried then paused to catch her breath. "I knew if we did not get off the road, you'd be dead," she squeaked quickly, before breaking down sobbing again.

Tam embraced her once more and whispered, "It's okay, Lenni. We're both fine." He held her until her sobs faded away.

As soon as he loosened his embrace, she threw her arms around his neck, knocked him onto the pallet, and kissed him franticly. Her hand rested on his chest as she lay across him, lips locked to his as he grabbed her shoulders and gently pushed her away.

Looking up at her beautiful face—cheeks flushed with excitement, swollen lips slightly parted as she gasped to catch her breath—Tam clinched his hand in an effort to control himself. "Lenni...love...please stop before I am unable to," he groaned, his heart beating wildly in his chest as she still lay on top of him.

"That's the thing, Tam. I don't want you to stop," she panted.

He positioned his arms around her waist and rolled her onto her back, then pushed up on his arms to where he hovered over her. He closed his eyes and took a deep breath before getting up and walking just outside the door. He leaned his back against the wall then turned around and banged his head on it three times before returning to the room.

Looking at her, he said, "Lenni, right now your emotions are running high. I have too much respect for you and your father to let things go any further than they already have, and if you have any love for me, you'll never let that happen again because I promise you, the next time, I will not stop," he warned her as he ran his hand through his hair.

Lenni's already swollen eyes watered as tears threatened to fall again. "Aren't you the one who said, we shouldn't feel guilty if we find ourselves in each other's arms?"

"I was mistaken to think it was only lust between us. You're so much more to me than that, and it's killing me to think that you're looking for someone else, and I'm stupid enough to help you find him," Tam continued, throwing his hands up in the air.

~~

Jael sat in the transport next to Sarik, her mind reeling as it tried to keep up with the wonders around her.

"Welcome to the city of Atlantis," Sarik told her.

As the transporter moved smoothly along the cobbled streets, Jael noticed there were others like Salima. Tall, long limbed, and skin the color of the sky. "Why do some of your people have blue skin?" she asked, looking out the window.

"They're not my people. They are Jinn, just as Salima is," he replied, not going into details.

Peeling her eyes from the windows, she glanced at Sarik before inquiring, "You have known my father since he was a boy, how is it you appear so young?"

"I'm not like you, Jael. My people roam the stars as yours do the land. Your lifespan is but a moment compared to ours," he explained.

"That's why you agreed to marry me? To you this is a moment of your life, an inconsequential token to accommodate a friend's request," she implied.

Fire blazed behind her eyes. There was something about her that made him want to know more. "Yes, it was one of the reasons I agreed," he answered, his voice laced with arrogance.

Jael sighed. As beautiful as he was, his dismissive attitude left her disheartened. "I see."

Sarik's heart sank—disappointed he may have hurt Jael's feelings. "But it was not the only reason." She was far more astute than Rowe claimed, and her beauty enthralled him.

Again her eyes made contact with his. It was a mistake she'd have to learn not to make. His beautiful blue eyes pierced right through her, melting her soul and making her forget his callousness. "I suppose we should both make the best of this situation, and I should be thankful you have come to my father's aid."

Sarik grinned. "Things are not always black and white, Jael. I believe you have the most to gain from this agreement, but only if you give me a chance, just as I am giving you."

"Forgive me for being a cynic, but I was raised to believe one day I'd be able to marry the man I love, and it has only been a week since my dreams were pulled out from under me," she sneered as the marvels around her were overshadowed by contempt.

An awkward silence fell, and for the first time in his life, Sarik's heart was wounded by rejection. He believed Jael would be like the others who fawned over him, kissing the ground he walked on. He regrouped his thoughts as his pride turned her dismissal to a game he would win. In a month's time, she would be eating out the palm of his hand. "I think this conversation has gotten off to a bad start. So, let us begin again. Welcome to Atlantis, Lady Jael. It would be my honor to show you its secrets if you would trust me," he said, holding his hand out to her as the transport stopped in front of the main headquarters of the city.

She took his offered hand and climbed out. Her heart skipped a beat as she looked up at the massive structure in front of her, its spires reaching to touch the clouds above it. The glass and metal reflected the sun almost blinded her before she walked into its shadows, following Sarik through moving glass doors. They walked into the well-lit room, and Jael noticed the lights did not flicker like the flames of a candle do. A man sat behind a short wall connected to a table, and as they approached he smiled

"Good afternoon, sir, is this the Lady Jael of Eir?" he asked as he touched the holo screen that hovered in front of him.

"Yes it is, Mr. Dobson. I'll see to her check-in personally, so don't bother to have the resource department send someone," Sarik said before heading towards the elevator.

As they approached the door, Jael stopped walking and clinched Sarik's hand tightly. He was taken aback when he could feel her fear as if it were his own. Normally, he could block such mundane emotions, but Jael's anxiety penetrated his wall and infiltrated his mind. "Jael, this is an elevator, it'll take us to the area where I live. Don't be afraid. It works much like the transport we rode over here on," he explained.

She released the death grip on his hand and followed him in. As it rose from the first floor, the wall behind them turned to glass windows. The further up it went, the more breath-taking the view. "It's the most beautiful thing I've ever seen. I feel like I'm flying." She laughed.

"Then you'll love the view from my quarters," he beamed.

The elevator slowed to a stop, the doors opened, and a set of large double doors came into view. Sarik walked to a panel on the wall next to the door and placed his hand on it. Like magic, the doors slid open revealing a large room with black shiny floors and a massive glass window that covered the entire outer wall. Jael walked around the room, her hands gently gliding across the different surfaces, feeling everything they came in contact with.

Sarik cleared his voice, breaking Jael's trance. "Would you like to see your room?"

Jael tilted her head and furrowed her brow. "Do we not sleep here by the fire?" She pointed to the enormous square fireplace in the center of the room surrounded by couches and cushions.

"No, Jael." He chuckled. "This is a living room. We gather with friends here, sort of like a great hall, but more private. Your room is over this way," he said, motioning toward a hallway.

She followed him to an ornate metal door and to its side was a panel much like the one on the outer door. Sarik fingered the pad then had Jael place her hand on it. As soon as she did, the door slid open quickly, causing her jump and back into Sarik.

"You should be able to open any of the doors in my quarters. If you need to lock the door, just place your finger over the red light and your hand on the pad. Don't worry about learning everything now, Salima will be here to help you," he explained.

Unlike the living room this room was light, and its walls were a pale shade of pearlescent pink reminiscent of the clouds at sunset. In the center of the room was a large, raised pallet with white spired corners and above it long lengths of pink and orange fabrics flowed from where the spires connected all the way down to the floor. The fabrics were like nothing she had ever seen. They were translucent, allowing the light to penetrate through them. The rug that covered the floor was soft under her feet and reached all the way to the walls. In one of the corners sat a raised cushioned platform with lots of pillows. "It's overwhelming, Sarik, and beyond anything I could ever imagine," she said.

"I take it you approve? I just had it redone for your arrival," he informed her. "Oh, I almost forgot, come this way," he said as he walked up to the door by the cushioned platform and opened it. "This is the bathroom."

"What is a bathroom?" she asked as she walked around the room.

"It's where you bathe and ...uh...mm...I'll let Salima explain," he stuttered, walking out of the bathroom quickly.

"I took the liberty of acquiring a new wardrobe for you. While you are here, you might want to dress accordingly, so you won't draw unnecessary attention," he said, walking to a door on the other side of the room and opening it. "If you'd like to pick some new clothes yourself, you have an allowance to get whatever you need, and I'm sure Salima will not mind taking you shopping."

"It's more than I could ever want. Thank you," she said, thumbing through the clothes in the closet.

"For the next month, I'll be one hundred percent at your disposal, Jael. Don't be afraid to ask me anything. I know this is a big adjustment." He smiled.

Chapter 7

After three days in Atlantis, Jael was about to go berserk. She had seen and learned so much in a short period of time her mind couldn't process anymore. Just when she thought she couldn't take one more new piece of information, Sarik introduced her to something called a bubble bath. She sank into the hot water until the fragrant bubbles tickled her nose. Lying back, she closed her eyes and purged her mind of all thoughts. Music played around her, the sound penetrating as every drumbeat resonated down to her bones. Stars appeared above her and beckoned her to dance with them as she started floating closer, darkness encompassing her.

Stretched out on the couch with his eyes closed, Sarik's thoughts wandered aimlessly before settling on Jael, then, without reason, panic struck. He jumped up from the couch and raced to Jael's locked bathroom door. "Override lock," he yelled at the door before it opened. He rushed to the large bathtub. He didn't see her, so he climbed in and frantically pushed the bubbles away, fishing for Jael underneath. Within seconds, he lifted her limp body out of the tub and laid her on the hard floor. Sarik yelled to the computer for a medic before he pinched her nose and placed his mouth over hers blowing a deep breath into her lungs. Water spewed from her mouth as the air left her lungs; he turned her on her side as she coughed.

Shaking from the adrenaline pumping through his body, he inhaled deeply then let it all out in one long breath. He wrapped a towel around her and carried her to bed just as the medics arrived.

When Jael opened her eyes, all she could see was Sarik's face, pale as ghost. The sound of people talking in the background buzzed around her. "What's going on?" She coughed as one of the medics wrapped her in a warm blanket.

"You almost drowned. The medics would like to monitor you to make sure you're alright," explained Sarik. He leaned over her and moved the wet tendrils from her face.

The other medic placed his hands over Jael, without touching her he slowly moved them from her head all the way to her feet. As he finished he said, "Everything looks good. There's still a little water in her lungs, but that's something I'm sure you can take care of," he said then looked at Jael. "Can you tell me what happened?"

As embarrassed as she was, Jael explained every detail of her bath.

The medic gave her an odd look. "Did you try to shape shift while you were in the water?"

"She's human. Why would you ask her that?" demanded Sarik.

"She's part human, but her physiology is eighty percent Jinn," he said, defending his question.

Sarik stood and pointed at the medic by the door. "You— find Salima and tell her I want her here now." Anger laced his voice.

"Yes, sir," he replied before dashing out the room.

Sarik paced the side of the bed and massaged his temples. "Jael, do you know how to shape shift?"

"I just learned to change into a cat a couple of months ago," she confessed. "How can I possibly be part Jinn?" Her body shook from the shock of everything.

Sarik looked at the remaining medic and said, "Thank you, I'll take it from here."

Jael coughed one last time, wrapped her arms around her knees, and rocked back and forth mumbling, "I can't be a Jinn. My dad's not a Jinn, my mom's not a Jinn, so how can I be part Jinn? My skin isn't blue. I can't be a Jinn," she repeated over and over, starring off into space.

Sarik looked back at Jael before he threw his hands up in the air and yelled, "Fuck!" He stormed out of the room and greeted Salima at the front door. "You have some serious explaining to do," he barked before she made it inside.

"What do you mean?" she asked calmly, as she walked to a couch and sat down.

"What games are you and Rowe playing? Did you not think it was important to let me know she was part Jinn?" he yelled as he postured in front of her.

Salima paused, looked Sarik in the eyes then sighed. "I wanted to tell you before the betrothal, but Rowe felt it would prevent you from marrying her. He made me swear not to say anything until a year after you wed."

"Damn straight it'll prevent me from marrying her!" he exclaimed. "Do you have any idea what the political consequences would be?" he asked, hands on his waist, pacing around the fire pit. "Grrr!" he screamed, kicking one of the vases near the couch half way across the room. Shards of glass sprayed throughout the area as the vase crashed against a nearby wall, and Salima winced.

"Calm down, Sarik. The business contract with Rowe is just that, a business contract. You only have to submit to their ceremony which is not binding here," she explained mater-of-factly.

Sarik plopped down on the couch next to Salima and snorted. "And what will your people say when they find out I refused to marry her legally after living with her as man and wife?" he asked, scooting to the edge of his seat, elbows on his thighs, and his head resting in hands.

"It was meant to stay secret, Sarik," Salima quietly answered.

He shot daggers at her then ran his hand through his hair. "The worst part of this mess is she had no idea." He pointed in the direction of Jael's room. "She's in the room right now having a mental breakdown after she almost drowned herself in the tub because no one saw fit to tell *her* the truth."

"You left her alone? God, Sarik, you're such an ass," she retorted as she pushed Sarik over with her hand and walked to Jael's room.

Jael still rocked back and forth mumbling to herself when Salima opened the door. Salima sat on the edge of the bed and put her arms around her. "It's okay," she crooned as she hugged her tight. Sarik was not far behind, but as he walked into the room, Salima gave him the look of death and said through gritted teeth, "Don't even think about it. You've done quite enough already."

Sarik fought the urge to punch something; he turned on his heels and left the room with his mind hashing over his current situation. "The solution is simple," he thought. "Her secret makes Rowe's contract null and void, so why am I angry?" His mind played back the moment he pulled her limp body out of the tub. Raw emotions overwhelmed him as if it were his own life in the balance. Frustration and confusion overflowed as he yelled and punched the metal wall; the bones shattered in his hand and left him crying on the floor.

The pain diverted his attention from the problem until Salima's voice penetrated his mind.

"Enough of your stupidity, Sarik. Tomorrow you better be ready to make things right with Jael, or you will have a Jinn problem on your hands!"

Sarik could feel Salima's anger and knew a response was neither necessary nor wanted. Grabbing his coat, he walked to one of the local bars and made himself comfortable. If pain could not silence the confusion that wracked his mind, then maybe inebriation would.

~~~

By morning Sarik's hand had repaired itself, which was more than he could say for his hangover and dilemma. Not yet ready for a confrontation, he left his quarters where Jael and Salima ate breakfast and walked to the general dining area. Sitting in the section reserved for higher ranking officers, Sarik ate alone. Before he finished he was joined by two mapping officers.

"Have you heard the news, sir? Your father decided to move Atlantis back to Enadlon."

"He's moving back to our home world?" Sarik questioned with raised brows.

"Yes, he's worried that we'll become a target, now that the Veshtu have landed the Olympus near Messenia."

"I thought Zeus was gone for good. Why he has returned? I do see my father's dilemma, especially after the war with the Jinn in India. Many of the refugees call Atlantis and Earth home and won't be very receptive to the move. Did he say when?"

"He awaits news from the Asgard. It should arrive in the next couple of months. Odin is going to settle the lands north of here and the captain wants to make sure any settlers who would like to stay have a place to go."

"Is the Valhalla also coming?" Sarik queried.

"Yes, Odin refused to settle the Asgard on Earth without the added protection of the Valhalla. I wish your father would request the protection of a battle cruiser instead of moving the Atlantis home—many of us would prefer to stay here," he added.

Sarik stood. "Thank you, gentlemen," Sarik said sarcastically.

Clinched fists and pursed lips, Sarik made his way to the captain's quarters. He pounded on the door until his father answered. "What have I done to piss you off?" Sarik asked as his father opened the door and let him in. They sat at the kitchen table across from each other, like two bulls waiting to lock horns. "It's a shame I should find out about the move from your mapping officers. Am I not worthy to attend a meeting of such importance?"

"It's not you, Sarik. It's that girl you intend to marry. She's is not what you think she is," grumbled Varen.

"I know exactly what she is—no thanks to you," Sarik argued. "How long did you plan to keep it secret, father? You knew the whole time I was negotiating with Rowe that she was part Jinn, and yet, you said nothing." He pointed finger at Varen.

"A mistake I regret," admitted Varen. "Look, son, the answer is simple. Her heritage is a breach of contract. Just send her back home," he suggested.

"It's not as simple as you think," admitted Sarik.

"It is to me. I can't afford to have issues with the Jinn right now. The Veshtu have returned, and the Jinn are our only allies here. You screw that girl over, and there'll be hell to pay. Get out while you still have your ass intact." Varen slammed his fists on the table.

"Do you mean to keep me from all meetings until I get rid of her?" Sarik asked.

"I'm telling you not to play with fire. You either send her home with her honor intact or make plans to spend the rest of your life with her. Your choice."

"I need to think," Sarik said as he stood to leave.

The lines on Varen's face loosened; he put his hand on Sarik's shoulder and offered him a moment of pity. "Mapping and Expedition is planning a trip north, and you need a break, Sarik. You should go with them and figure this out."

Sarik turned to face his father. "I'll think about it, but I could only go for a few days."

The crux of the matter set in. As much as his father's words hurt, he was right. A temporary relationship with Jael would not go unnoticed by the Jinn. It would have to be all or nothing, which was not something he planned for. He was already emotionally invested in her, maybe even in love, another unforeseen event. First he had to get back in Jael's good graces. He treaded in uncharted territory; love was as foreign to him as indoor plumbing was to Jael. Sarik headed back to his quarters. He had no idea what he was going to say to Jael, but anything was better than the nothing he left her with this morning.

"Jael," he yelled, craning his head around to look for her. To his dismay, she was not there and neither was Salima. "Where in the hell are they?" he said aloud. Disappointed by their absence, he walked to M & E and added his name to the manifest—maybe a trip away would do him some good.

~~~

Jael followed Salima through the narrow alley. They headed to the charterhouse established for refugee Jinn. Although Salima knew about Jael's life, she didn't know the circumstance of her conception. It was a subject Varen had been unwilling to share with her, so they would have to dig for answers from the ground up. Upon their arrival, they were greeted by an old friend of Salima's.

"It's been too long since your last visit, Salima," said the woman as they hugged.

"I've missed your company too—something I hope to remedy soon. Unfortunately, today I'm here for business and not pleasure. Do you have any information on recent Jinn cross breeding activities?" Salima asked.

"We have a few records of attempts to interbreed with humans, but as far as I can see, we haven't had much success." The woman pawed through the records.

Salima smiled. "I think your success is debatable. What do you have from eighteen years ago?"

"Three separate attempts were made that year with different surrogates; all of them used the same male sample. We don't show any of them as successful." She looked over at the young girl next to Salima, it wasn't hard to see from her long lithe body, and golden eye color, that she was part Jinn.

"Is Mila of Eir one of the surrogates?" asked Salima.

"No, but oddly enough we do have information that she was implanted. The male donor is different than the others, and we have no information past the implant procedure. It was assumed the implant didn't take," the woman said, eyeing Jael once more.

"What do you have on the male donor?"

She searched her holo screen, and after a few moments a quizzical look crossed her brow. "This is really bizarre. The male donor is listed as *origin*. I have no idea what that means." She shook her head. "It looks like the attending for the procedure was Kali."

Salima rolled her eyes to the ceiling and sighed. "Anyone else?"

"There's no secondary listed, although I'm sure there would have been." She stated taping on the screen. "You know Kali's track record. Her genetic experiments caused far too many deaths. I'm surprised they let her do the procedure to begin with."

"That certainly brings to light the sudden death of Jael's mother during child birth. If you could please ask around and find out what was meant by *origin*, I would really appreciate it. Thank you for your help," said Salima.

After she said goodbye, Salima and Jael headed back to headquarters. As they walked along the cobbled road, Salima glanced at Jael and said, "It appears we have found more questions than answers."

"At least I know for sure that I'm part Jinn. What I don't understand is how my father expects Sarik and I to rule as heirs when neither of us have a blood connection to him."

"That's most likely his main reason for not telling anyone, including you," Salima said.

They walked down the alleyway, Jael's mind wandered between random thoughts, when out of the blue she commented. "I don't know what to do. I want to love Sarik, but he confuses me."

Salima laughed at Jael's random remark. "Sarik confuses everyone."

Jael chuckled. "That's no way to reassure me he'll make a good husband."

"I never said he would," Salima teased.

"Every time I look into those blue eyes, my body quivers. Then he does something selfish or hurtful, and it's like a kick to the stomach. I don't know how he knew I was drowning, but he did. If you could've seen the look on his face when he saved me, you'd be confused too. One minute he looks at me like I'm his world, and the next he abandons me when I need him most."

"I have known Sarik a long time, and the one thing I am certain about is he knows nothing about love. He may be a fine specimen of the male persuasion and without a doubt will make you the envy of every woman in the clan—and Atlantis for that matter—but a thoughtful man he is not," Salima told her.

"Thoughtful or not, I have to do what is best for the clan. I'll spend an eternity with this heartless, but completely gorgeous man if it'll bring protection to my people," Jael vowed.

"There's one little problem, Jael. Now that he knows you're part Jinn, he can't enter casually into a marriage. He never intended to make this union anything other than a business contract between him and Rowe," she explained.

"Where does that leave me?"

"You can either forget the whole betrothal or convince Sarik he wants to spend the rest of his life with you, which, by the way, is a very, very long time."

"I need to get away from here and do some soul searching, but I'm not ready to go home," confessed Jael.

Salima thought for a few minutes then suggested, "There's a Mapping and Expedition trip going north tomorrow. I'm sure there'll be room for one more. I can have you added to the manifest when we get to headquarters."

"Will I get to ride on a sky ship?" Her eyes opened wide with excitement.

"Yes, you'll get to ride in a shuttle, and you'll also get to freeze your butt off in the cold. They sleep in tents due to the isolation of the areas they're exploring. They stay as far away as possible from any human settlements, so they don't panic the aboriginal populous," she explained.

"I know what you mean. I remember the first time I heard the dragon from Hy-Brasil in the woods." She laughed, thinking back to how ignorant she was. "It nearly scared me to death."

"I'll see that you have the necessary clothing and supplies on the shuttle," said Salima.

"Are you not going with me?"

"As much as I would love too, Jael, I already have plans. Don't worry. The people who work in that department are really nice and will take care of you," Salima reassured Jael.

"I'm so excited. I don't know how I'm going to sleep tonight!" she exclaimed, skipping and laughing.

"Whatever you do, don't tell Sarik about your trip. He'll be furious if he finds out I have allowed you to go on a Mapping and Expedition trip," Salima warned.

Salima arranged a transport to take Jael to the shuttle, two hours before departure. *That should be plenty of time for her to leave without being noticed by Sarik,* she thought. Afraid Jael's excitement might cue Sarik that there was something up, Salima sent her to retrieve her bow from the armory and drop it off at M & E—the trip on foot would take more than an hour. In the meantime, she slipped off to Sarik's quarters.

Sarik's sat on a leather cushioned couch, the flames of the large, square fire pit in the center of the floor danced as he stared, lost in his own thoughts. "I didn't see you come in," he said to Salima.

"You like her, don't you?" Salima laughed as she sat on a couch on other side of the fire.

"It's not funny, Salima," he barked across the fire. "It was not part of the deal. This was a business contract, not an emotional one—especially my emotions," he shot before standing to fix himself a drink.

"I would say I feel sorry for you, but I've seen the way you've treated women the last couple hundred years, and honestly, it serves you right to fall for the one you weren't supposed to fall for."

He fixed two glasses of Cerulean Ale and handed one to Salima as he sat on the couch next to her. "I don't know how to explain it. There's something about Jael that draws me in like dust to a black hole."

Salima sipped her drink; the blue liquid tickled her tongue as it evaporated quicker than she could swallow. "Maybe it's the fact that she doesn't feel the same way about you and being rejected keeps you enamored? How fast will you lose interest if she falls for you?" she asked.

"I need time to myself. I'm leaving tomorrow to go north with M & E, please let Jael know after I leave. I don't want to waste time explaining everything to her."

"Running away, are you? And from a woman no less," she teased.

"Yes, yes I am," he replied, downing his entire drink and fixing another one.

"Wow, Sarik, I've never seen you toil over anything. This must be serious if your ego hasn't solved the problem."

He plopped down on the couch and rolled his eyes. "Haha...I'm feeling like a cornered space rat, even my father is pressuring me. Now that I think about it, by the time I left he almost seemed in favor of the union," he said, cocking his head to the side in thought then quickly shaking it off.

"Your father? The one who almost killed you when he caught you and Tal having too much fun is in favor of you marrying a human Jinn? Now I know you've been drinking too much." She laughed, then handed him her empty glass.

Eyeing her empty glass, he shrugged his shoulders, and finished the rest of his drink. He fixed them each another, looked down at the two glasses he just filled, and paused for a moment before tossing back the contents of both and refilling them again. Handing Salima her drink, he sat down next to her again. They chatted for twenty minutes before Sarik raised his glass. "A toasss!" he slurred, his blue eyes glossed over like frozen lakes. "To runnin' away, may the solusson be found before I am." He swallowed his drink and stood, his legs wobbling as he attempted to keep his balance.

Putting her glass on the end table, Salima slung Sarik's arm around her neck and carried him to his room. She sat him at the foot of his bed and pulled back his blankets. By the time she arranged the covers, Sarik had already taken off his clothes.

"Have you no shame," she grumbled. His limp arm over her shoulder and her arm around his naked waist, she helped him to the side of the bed.

"You're ssso preddy," he slurred as she sat him on the edge of the bed.

"And if you don't remove your hand from my breast, jackass, you're going to be seeing two of me," she calmly stated, removing his hand and pushing him back onto the bed.

"Love you too," he garbled before passing out.

Salima let sighed as she left his room, shutting the door behind her. He would be too drunk to catch Jael leaving in the wee hours of the morning. The moment she made it back to the living room, the front door opened.

Jael returned from her errand and asked, "Is Sarik home?"

"Yes, he's asleep already. I have to go, so have a good trip. I'll see you when you get back," Salima said from the doorway, eager to leave.

Chapter 8

Lenni shivered and pulled her shawl tighter around her shoulders. The wind howled and whistled between the sails of the boats on the dock. She quickened her pace attempting to keep up with Tam's stride, but her feet were blistered from days of walking the streets of Blackrock looking for her dream man.

"Tam, slow down," she yelled against the wind.

He stopped and looked back at her. "I have work to do, and you're holding me up."

"My feet are blistered."

"I told you to stay in the room and give up this search. But, did you listen? No. You followed me out into the cold to look for this man. So, forgive me if I lack the sympathy you're looking for. You're not going to get any from me as long as you continue this search."

Lenni sat on the breakwall and removed her shoes. The cold cobblestones dulled the pain in her aching feet, but did nothing for the chill that penetrated the rest of her. Tam's anger hit her like the icy squall that surrounded them, making her eyes water.

As much as Tam wanted to be unsympathetic, the distress painted on Lenni's face pained him. His face softened, he took a deep breath, then sat next to her and clasped her frozen hands. "Let's go back to the inn and get you warmed up."

He carried her back and ordered lunch. After they ate, Tam ordered Lenni back to the room. She hung her head in defeat as she padded her way down the hall, realizing what she asked of Tam was more than any man should have to endure. She was no closer to finding her mystery man than she was two weeks ago when they arrived in Blackrock. The only thing she managed to find was that Tam had the patience of a saint, and she was testing every last ounce of it. She sat on the edge of the bed, wrapped herself in a blanket, and stared at the stack of wood by the fireplace too cold to get up and start the fire.

A few minutes later, Tam arrived with a bucket of hot water and a small bag of scented salt. He placed the bucket by her feet and added the salt before starting the fire in the hearth. "I thought you might want to soak your feet. The salt is supposed to help them heal."

Lenni closed her eyes and inhaled the lavender scented steam drifting from the bucket, before inching her feet into the hot water and letting out a sigh. Tam leaned against the wall with his elbow, and poked at the kindling with a stick. Mindlessly, she stared at his tall muscular body wondering how she missed that he was no longer the awkward lanky boy she once knew. He had grown into a man—a kind, thoughtful, patient man that any woman in her right mind would kill for the chance to have his attention. It was time for her to let go of her childish dreams of finding her mysterious, would-be soul mate and focus on the here and now. Tears fell down her face as she mentally let go of her dreams and resigned herself to love Tam.

Without warning, Tam was overwhelmed with confusion and sadness. He glanced at Lenni, tears streaming down her face and realized that it was her emotions that he felt.

Balancing the stick against the wall, he sat next to her on the bed. He placed his hand on her cheek, pulling her to face him as he wiped her tears with his thumb.

Lenni clasped Tam's hand on her cheek. She closed her eyes then kissed his palm. A lump formed in her throat as she looked into his beautiful green eyes. All of the feelings for Tam she had been suppressing came rushing in; the floodgate was open and there would be no going back.

There was something different about the way Lenni looked at him. Compelled, he leaned over and gently kissed her lips. Lenni's desire filled the void that was left from years of yearning for Wren. It was real this time and not of his own longing for happiness. He smiled as pulled away from her, his hand caressing her face.

"I'm done looking for something that's right here in front of me." She squeezed his hand. Her eyes welled with fresh tears, and she took a deep breath before smiling at Tam.

"Do you truly mean it, Lenni? Because at this moment, you hold my heart on a thread."

"Your heart is right here next to mine," she said, putting her hand over her chest. "Feel." She dropped her hand then moved his hand to rest on her chest as her heart raced against it.

Fighting overwhelming lust, he kissed her cheek before he got up from the edge of the bed and stood in front of her, his feet straddling the bucket of water. He lifted her chin so her eyes met his. Lost in pools of blue, he paused for a moment. "And that's exactly where I want it to be." He kissed her one last time then sat in one of the chairs across from the bed.

The water in the bucket had cooled to the same fridged temperature of the room. Lenni remove her feet from the water and dried them. Still wrapped in the blanket, she walked over to the fire and stood shivering. Tam walked up behind her and wrapped his arms around her shoulders. His body warmed her back. She could imagine the rest of her life wrapped up in his arms. For the first time in her life, she was truly happy.

He kissed the top of her head and let go his embrace. "There's a storm brewing and I still have a couple of your father's ships I need to check on. Will you be okay by yourself?"

"Yes, I'll be fine—cold, but fine."

Tam put on his coat and looked back at her from the doorway. "As soon as your feet heal and the storm clears we'll go to the dressmakers and check on your and Halis' gowns. If they're done, and it's okay with you, I'd like to head home."

"I'm very much ready to go home." She grabbed the back of the chair and pulled it before the fire then sat.

"I should be back in a couple of hours. If you need anything, just tell the innkeeper's daughter when she comes to get the water bucket."

"I'll be fine...Now go already. I can't miss you if you don't leave," she teased.

Tam smiled and closed the door behind him. He braced himself before he opened the outside door to the inn, wincing as pellets of ice hit his face. When he approached, he could see the white caps that formed on the usually placid harbor. The boats rolled from side to side rubbing against the dock that moored them. Refusing to let the foul weather put a damper on his mood, Tam made his way to one of the boats. The crew swiftly removed their cargo as Tam jumped on to the deck and greeted the captain.

"Tam, what brings you to Blackrock in such weather?" said the captain before yelling at his crew to make haste.

"I was headed this way, so Rowe asked me to check on his ships. How are things going?'

"Besides the rough seas, things go well. We just got back from Hem, but I hear there are problems in the south. A Beaker ship and its cargo were captured to the south by raiders—they killed the entire crew. Damn barbarians are making it difficult for the Beakers to trade with us."

"Patrol ships and costal guards are organizing as we speak. The Lairds hope to have this problem taken care of soon."

"I suggest we take this conversation to the inn. The crew is done unloading and this forsaken cold is making my bones ache."

"That sounds like a great idea. I'll tell the other captains and meet you there."

The meeting with the ships' captains lasted longer than Tam expected, and it was late by the time he returned to the room. The fire was almost dead and the room cold, so he added a hand full of kindling to the coals and a couple of logs. Lenni was sound asleep balled up under the blanket including the ones from his bed. Unwilling to sleep in a cold bed without a blanket as hell froze over outside and drafted into the room, he stripped down and crawled under the covers with Lenni. He attempted to keep his distance in the small bed, but cold air he let under the blanket when he snuck under caused Lenni to shiver and cuddle right up against him. The scent of lavender drifted off her arm as it lay across his bare chest. Before long her leg made its way on top of his. He would've moved to his own bed if not for Lenni's welcomed warmth.

Tam's mind drifted in and out of sleep throughout the night. He tried to block his physical needs from his thoughts, but Lenni's warm breath against his neck was almost too much for him.

Dawn crept in through the cracks in the shutters. Lenni stretched her leg then curled it back up before becoming fully aware of Tam's naked body beneath her. Her cheeks turned red, she turned to her side, and moved away, but not before Tam wrapped his arms around her waist and pulled her back against his chest. She could feel his hardness against the small of her back, let out an audible gasp and writhed.

"Please stop moving," he whispered in her ear.

"We can't do this," she pleaded softly.

He let out a yawn then replied, "We aren't going to do anything, unless you continue to arouse me with your wiggling."

Curiosity was getting the best of her. She stopped moving and leaned closer, feeling all of his virility through her shift. She reached her arm in back of her and laid her hand on his muscular thigh.

He intertwined his fingers with hers then moved her arm back in front of her. He lightly trailed kisses down the back of her neck, before stopping. Tam released her hand, let out a deep breath, and rolled over onto his back and away from her.

Lenni turned over and propped herself up on her elbow facing him. "Did I do something wrong?"

Tam looked up at the ceiling. "On the contrary, but your dad would not appreciate the molestation of his daughter," he said and faced her.

"You have a good point, although, he'll most likely have your head for sleeping naked with her anyway," she said, raising her brow.

"Are you suggesting I continue to assault you because I'm screwed regardless?"

"Yep, pretty much." She ran her fingers lightly down his chest before his hand stopped hers at his waist.

"Tempting—but no." He swung his legs over the side of the bed and pulled one of the blankets around his waist to hide himself from Lenni's curious eyes.

Lenni continued to ogle. His body was nothing short of breathtaking. Every well-formed muscle cast a shadow on his body in the stormy morning light. Had she seen him naked sooner, she might not have wasted so much time pining for an imaginary man.

Tam watched her staring at him as if hypnotized. He cleared his throat to get her attention and motioned for her to turn her head so he could change. Lenni frowned before looking away.

"I want a summer wedding with lots of flowers."

He tied his leather pants and threw the blanket back on the bed. "Who said anything about getting married?"

Lenni turned around, the stunned look on her face caused Tam to give a big belly laugh. "I'm just kidding. A summer wedding sounds beautiful. But we'll have to behave ourselves until then." She jumped up out of bed and threw her arms around him. He could feel every inch of her through the thin fabric. "Not helping," he groaned.

She released her embrace and backed away from him. "I'm so sorry." She laughed.

The sheerness of her shift caught Tam off guard. His face turned red as he quickly turned away and ran his fingers through his hair. "Good god woman, put some clothes on before you make me do something stupid."

"I was thinking the same thing," she said, throwing his shirt at him from across the room and hitting him in the back of the head.

～～

It was three days before the storm passed and the weather warmed. Lenni neatly packed her new dress in her saddlebag leaving little room for the rest of her belongings. The dress was a beautiful pale blue with silver trim. She intended to wear it to Jael's wedding, but Tam's face lit up the moment he saw her in it at the dressmakers, so she decided to save it for her own wedding. Their departure from Blackrock was bitter sweet. She learned so much about Tam the last few days shut up in the room with him, that she wished the storm had lasted longer.

"Are you ready to go?" Tam asked from the doorway.

"Could you carry a few of my things in your bag? I couldn't fit everything in mine."

Lenni closed the clasp on her bag and handed it to Tam. "Did you get new directions to Edric's? I have no desire to get shot at again."

"Yes, and we'll actually have an escort there. There are a couple of soldiers from Monmalor who just finished patrol duty and were headed that way. They said they'd be more than happy for the company. Although they might change their mind if they have to wait much longer for us to leave." Lenni grabbed the last of her belongings and followed Tam to the stable where their escort waited.

The half-day's ride to Dunfin was uneventful. Laird Dunfin waited for their arrival with bad news from Halor. Lenni and Tam sat next to each other on a bench clasping hands.

"I hate to be the bearer of bad news, so I will just come right out and say it. Rowe is dead, and Dugun has assumed the duties of Laird of Eir."

Lenni let out an ear piercing cry. Tam gasped and clinched his chest as her mental anguish impaled everyone around her. As soon as he regained his composure, he put his arm around Lenni's shoulder and pulled her close.

Tam looked at Laird Dunfin. "Do you know how he died?"

"Dugun is trying to play it off as natural causes, but everyone suspects poisoning. He isn't allowing the priestess to take the body and confirm that."

Tam massaged his temple with his free hand. "We need to get home and fast. Are Ugis and Edric ready to ride?"

"They are preparing the horses as we speak. Your father has sent Rowe's captain of the guard and a small escort to get you, so you'll have to wait. I'm expecting them here later tonight."

Lenni looked up from Tam's chest, her eyes red and puffy, but her mood calmer. "Dugun can't be laird. Everything father has worked for will be destroyed," she said as if to plead to Tam to do something.

"I need to talk to my father. There has to be a reason the clan has not protested his claim." Tam's eyes watered as it all sank in. Rowe had been like a second father to him, and now he was gone.

Laird Dunfin clasped Tam's shoulder. "Let your father know if he needs anything, he has my full support."

Lady Dunfin entered the room with a pitcher of wine and cups for Tam and Lenni.

Lenni took a few sips and began to cry again. Lady Dunfin took the cup from her hand and placed it on the table. She put her arms around Lenni and petted her hair. "It's okay, my dear, let it all out."

Tam swallowed what was in his cup then walked to the stable where Edric and Ugis were getting ready for the trip home.

Ugis threw his arms around his brother when he walked in. "I'm glad you and Lenni made it here safely. I heard about the attempt on your life on the way to Blackrock."

"I'm glad our trip back was far less eventful." Tam took the brush from Ugis hand and began to brush Farth.

Edric walked outside the stable and returned with a small pouch in his hand. "I believe this is for you. I found it in the stable at Halor, but didn't know it was yours until I showed it to Ugis a couple of days ago."

Opening the pouch, Tam eyed the necklace he intended to give to Lenni before she ran off. "Thank you. I know just what to do with this." He walked back to the house. Lenni was still on the bench, her cheeks flush from the wine. He took the necklace out of the pouch and put it around Lenni's neck.

Her fingers touched the metal pendant that hung from the leather cord. "It's beautiful."

"I stayed up making it for you the night you kissed me in the great hall. I tried to give it to you the next day, but you had already rejected me."

She stood and threw her arms around his neck. "I love you," she whispered.

"I love you too. We'll make it through this together."

"I know."

Chapter 9

Jael tiptoed to the front door and placed her hand on the pad. The door opened with a loud swoosh, heightening her nervousness as she scurried down the hall to the elevator. It was still dark and the cold air bit into her as she ran from the comfort of the warm building to the transport. At the shuttle, the Mapping and Expeditions officer, Captain Ross, checked her in and handed her the gear Salima ordered.

Jael quickly walked to the bathroom and changed. She eyed herself in the mirror. Her thin crew uniform left her feeling naked, but far warmer than she had been. The new clothes also allowed her to blend in with the rest of the crew. So, for the sake of being incognito, she'd suffer through her embarrassment. She would be Jael, M & E crew member, and would perform duties just like the rest. Taking a deep breath for courage, she walked back to the shuttle and reported to Captain Ross.

During the flight she would learn about topographical imaging from one of the other crew members who had yet to arrive. She helped the others load the shuttle with the equipment they needed for this trip.

Sunlight filtered onto the runway as the last of the cargo was loaded. Captain Ross checked the manifest one last time for all his passengers, and one person was still missing. The

Captain said he couldn't wait any longer, so everyone boarded the shuttle and took their assigned seats. Sitting in the back, Jael followed what the other crew members did and fastened her seatbelt. Just as the shuttle was about to takeoff, the outside door near the cockpit opened, and their lone straggler boarded the shuttle and promptly went inside the cockpit with the Captain before Jael could get a look.

In the terminal, Varen stood next to Salima watching the shuttle take-off. "Do you think it will work?" Varen asked.

"I hope so," she replied, eyes glued on the ship moving across the sky. Once it was gone, she turned to Varen. "I have to admit this has been one of your more cleaver plans. I never thought reverse psychology would work on him." Salima half smiled at his deceit.

"Now, if my idiot son could see his nose in front of his face before he runs out of time," Varen growled.

"There's only so much we can do," she sighed.

~~~

Not long after the shuttle took-off, the crew unbuckled their seatbelts and moved about freely. Jael made her way to the front, eager to see if her instructor had arrived at the last minute. As soon as she reached the cockpit door, it opened and Sarik stood in front of her. "What are you doing here?" Wide eyed and brow furrowed, Jael crossed her arms and waited for his response.

"I was about to ask you the same question," he claimed as he moved back into the cockpit and motioned for Jael to enter.

"Let me guess. You're going to teach the new crew member topographical imaging?" She followed him into the cockpit.

"Why do I get the distinct feeling we've been set up?" Sarik chuckled.

Before she could reply, Captain Ross chimed in, "How is it that everyone on this crew knew you were being set up and you didn't?"

Sarik shook his head and rolled his eyes to Jael. "I finally figured out what my father and Salima were getting at, Jael. It appears they're playing match-makers, and you and I are their targets." He sat in the co-pilots chair next to Captain Ross.

Jael sat on the large cushioned ledge behind the captain's seat. "Why would they want to? From what Salima told me, your father is against the betrothal."

He turned his chair to face her. He had not realized how captivating Jael was. Her crew uniform clung to every inch of her body as her long, graceful legs stretched out in front her. Beautiful red, waist-length hair framed her face, accentuating her emerald-green eyes and perfect lips that turned up at the corners. He scanned every inch of her body and wondered how he could've overlooked her more striking qualities.

Jael blushed as she became painfully aware of Sarik's ogling and looked down at the floor in embarrassment, breaking the trance Sarik was under.

"My father suffers from my-son-has-been-a-bachelor-for-too-long syndrome." He laughed.

"I'm serious, Sarik. Where does that leave us?" she asked, crossing her arms in front of her.

"On a Mapping and Expedition trip and not for the reasons we thought we were going." He chuckled, not knowing how to address her real concern.

His answer was met with silence, after a moment he added, "I think we need a clean slate. I'll promise not to be a self-absorbed ass if you promise to base your decision on your affections and not the needs of your clan." He stretched out his hand to shake on it.

When her pause lasted too long and became awkward, Sarik raised his brow and shot her a playful grin. Just as he was about to give up and retract his hand, she reached out and sealed the deal. In his excitement, he stood, still clasping her hand, and kissed her. The crew in the back whooped and clapped, prompting Sarik to kick the door shut and kiss her again.

Jael pulled away from his grasp, heart beating fast, and leaned against the ledge she had been sitting on. She felt like her knees would buckle. His kiss left her dizzy, so she closed her eyes as the world swirled around her.

Honest concern imbued his voice when he asked, "Are you okay?"

She fluttered her eyes open, but the twinkles that flashed before her turned to gray and then darkness. The tension melted from her body as she slid to the floor.

Sarik knew there was something wrong the minute her eyes rolled to the back of her head. He scooped her up before she hit the ground and placed her in his seat before opening the door and yelling for smelling salt. "Well, that's the first time a mere kiss from me has made a woman faint," he confessed to Captain Ross, who sat in his chair shaking his head.

"Didn't you just promise not to be a self-absorbed ass?" He laughed at Sarik's expression as the medic ran in with a vile of smelling salt.

Sarik gently waved it under Jael's nose while the medic monitored her vitals. "It only count's when the promised person is conscious," he reasoned.

The pungent odor wafted under her nose and Jael's limbs flailed. She gasped and opened her eyes wide.

"Hello, sunshine." Sarik winked at her as he waved off the medic. "I think you've had too much excitement for one day." He threw her over his shoulder and carried her to one of the beds used for emergencies. The entire crew watched their every move as if they were animals at a zoo. Sarik was used to attention, but could have done without it at the moment.

Trying to sit, Jael lifted her head and sighed, falling heavily back down on the pillow.

Clasping her hand, Sarik chided, "Just rest, I don't need you passing out on me again."

"I guess I was overwhelmed," she groggily moaned.

Sarik opened his mouth to reply. Jael turned her head and raised her brow before the words left his mouth. He paused for a moment then said, "I still need to teach you how to use the imaging system," instead of "I have that effect on women."

After several minutes Jael was able to sit up without feeling light-headed, so Sarik called the medic to the back to check her over once more, before allowing her to get up. Concluding that her body was just getting used to the manifestation of her powers, the medic cleared her for duty.

Jumping down from the bed, Jael followed Sarik to the imaging area. She ignored the stares and murmurs of the other crew members as she walked staring straight ahead.

Sarik read her uneasiness and audibly cleared his throat in disapproval. The crew dispersed and resumed their duties.

"This is the imaging computer." Sarik ran his hands across the clear glass panel that sat waist high in front of him. "It works like your holo computer. You bring up the screen in front of you like this." He showed her, moving his hands across the holo portion of the screen. He explained in detail how to use the computer and felt Jael reaching into his mind and soaking in everything he knew about the system. Surprised by her ability to process and mimic his thoughts, Sarik realized she picked up on this operation quicker than he did—a quality he oddly found attractive, despite his competitive nature.

Soon they landed in a large level meadow isolated from any local population, and the crew started to unload the supplies. Captain Ross spouted orders and organized their priorities for the remainder of the day. Jael grabbed her bow and led a small party into the heavily pined forest to find wood while Sarik helped to pitch tents. She marveled at Sarik's ability to accept orders, despite his elevated rank. He always knew when to lead and when to follow, a trait many leaders lacked and something she had not expected.

Once night fell and everyone had eaten, the crew members left the warmth of the fire and retreated to their tents. Jael had no idea where she was going to sleep. There was never a conversation about sleeping arrangements as there had been for everything else, from the food to the outhouse. So, she sat near the fire by herself for several minutes before Sarik peeked his head out of the tent and asked, "Jael, are you coming to bed?"

Too tired to protest sharing shelter with Sarik, she entered the tent. It was warmer than she expected inside. There was only one bed, and by the look on Sarik's face, she was expected to share that with him. She stood by the tent opening not knowing what to do.

"Are you coming to bed? Or do you plan on standing there all night, letting the cold air in?" he asked, unaware of the problem.

She quickly closed the tent. "Sarik, I can't sleep in the same bed as you."

"Jael, either climb into bed with me or share a tent with one of the other crew members. There are no spare beds, so you'll have to make do," he stated. "I promise I won't bite." He sat up and allowed the blanket to fall off of him.

She rolled her eyes, but when she glanced back down, she got more than an eye full and turned away quickly. Jael let out a deep breath; the sight of Sarik's naked body bored into her mind, only increasing her nervousness.

"Here, if it'll make you feel better, I'll put on pants," he compromised. He walked up to Jael, who had her back to him, and placed his hands on her shoulders then whispered in her ear, "You're exhausted and need sleep. I promise not to do anything, so will you please come to bed?" He handed her one of his shirts and climbed back into bed.

Unwilling to sleep in her dirty uniform, she cleared her throat and motioned him to turn away. Stripping down to her underclothes, she put on the shirt Sarik gave her before climbing into bed. She faced the outer wall of the tent with her back to him, trying to ignore the fact she was in bed with a man. The wind howled outside the tent, and Jael shivered. Sarik wrapped his arms around her and pulled her closer to his warm body.

Mentally, she wanted to protest his closeness, but she was too tired and too cold to make the effort. She attempted to make the best of it and relax her back against the warmth of his chest.

He laid his head in the crook of her neck and whispered, "You're a Jinn for Pete's sake, could you please make some heat before you shake me right out of this tent?"

"I don't know how," she whispered back, his warm breath on the back of her neck making her shake even more.

He laced his fingers with hers and made more heat than he was already generating. Sarik lazily whispered back, "Reach into my mind like you did when I was teaching you the imaging system. Feel the way my body produces heat when I make the energy around it move faster."

Drifting into his mind, she saw the way he manipulated the energy. Mimicking him, her chilled bones started to warm, and soon the process became involuntary as she drifted off to sleep with Sarik's hand still laced with hers.

By morning they were drenched in sweat. "I'm going to have to teach you to control that," Sarik grumbled as he went from being cooked to freezing the second he crawled out from under the blankets. "God's tits, it's cold in here," he cried. "Is it any wonder the locals believe in a frozen hell?"

"Just be happy I didn't catch the tent on fire." She laughed.

"You've caught on to everything so quick. I'm starting to forget that you were not born to our ways," he admitted as he passed her clothes to her.

"As odd as it sounds, sometimes I feel as if I were born into your world and not mine. I'm more comfortable with your technology than I am with Eir's lack of."

"When you look inside a person's mind, it's hard to discriminate between their feelings and memories and yours," he warned before quickly cleaning his teeth.

Something struck Sarik as being off, the moment he stepped out of his tent. Within seconds it registered the shuttle was missing, but the captain was still there. "Captain Ross, where's the shuttle?" he asked, more out of curiosity than panic.

"We don't need it. It'll be back in two weeks to pick us up, so don't get your panties in a bunch."

"Two weeks?" he barked loud enough for the whole camp to hear.

"Yes, Prince Sarik, two weeks," he replied calmly, taking a sip of his coffee completely unmoved by Sarik's panicked observance.

"How in God's name am I supposed to keep a platonic relationship with Jael if she's sleeping half on top of me every night?" Sarik ran his fingers through his hair and paced.

"Sounds like a personal problem," replied the captain, before walking away.

Drawn to the ruckus Sarik caused, Jael approached him. "What's wrong?"

Lips pursed, Sarik relayed the Captain's message. "Two weeks in the middle of nowhere and no shuttle."

"How are we supposed to do topographical imaging without the imaging equipment?"

"My point exactly," he scoffed.

"I can't spend two weeks doing nothing."

"If I have my way, we won't," he replied, storming off to find the Survey Officer.

Jael shrugged off Sarik's anger and located a group about to leave for the day to gather mineral samples. They were more than happy to have her help, since she proved to be invaluable when it came to survival in the woods.

After three days of Sarik and Jael going in different directions, Captain Ross forbid the crews to allow them on any further missions, which set Sarik off once more. He grabbed a small tent, some supplies, and a survey pack then headed into the woods.

～～

After the first week, Captain Ross called into headquarters to let them know that M & E finished their primary mission. Unfortunately their secondary mission was a complete failure. Sarik and Jael were no closer to being in love with one another than they were when they got there. It was time to execute plan "B". Captain Ross pulled Sarik and Jael into his tent for a meeting. "I have a job for you two," claimed the captain. "We've not been able to get good information on this valley over here," he said, pointing on the map to an area ten miles from camp. "And I don't have enough people to make the hike there right now. Could you and Jael take the survey equipment and get us some ground readings?" he asked.

"Finally, something productive to do," Sarik said, agreeing to take the job.

"We'll take it," sang Jael in her excitement.

"Good. And if you leave within the hour, you'll have time to make it there and back before nightfall," the Captain suggested.

Checking the survey gear one last time before they left camp, Sarik closed the lid and tied it to the bottom of his pack. They followed a lower ridge until they got to the valley marked on the map. He and Jael surveyed the area then hiked back to camp. They were about a mile away when Sarik sensed there was something wrong. They should've been able to hear talking or the constant hum of the solar generator, but Sarik could hear nothing. As soon as he stepped out of the woods he saw why. "Are you fucking kidding me!" he yelled at the top of his lungs to the empty camp.

Plopping down in what used to be the center of camp, Jael's exhausted look and frown spoke volumes.

Sitting beside her, he clasped her cold hands between his as the snow fell. The fire was not going to start by itself, and they needed heat. Sarik got up and stacked a pile of wood in the pit at the circles center. When he was done, Jael started the fire and they moved closer to the heat. Jael sat down on the log and removed her wet boots and socks. She placed them by the fire to dry, and attempted to massage the circulation back into her blistered feet. Sarik limped to where the previsions were and filled the kettle with water. He grabbed two meal packs before returning to the fire beside Jael. After placing the kettle on a small metal rack on the edge of the flames, Sarik sat down next to Jael and handed her one of the meal packs. She placed the pack unopened on the log, got up, and knelt in front of Sarik to remove his boots for him.

He put his hand on hers to stop her. "Jael, you don't have to do that."

Exhausted, she looked up. "I know, but I want to." She placed his boots and socks next to hers by the fire before sitting back down next to him.

After they finished eating their cold supper, they sat on the ground in front of the log wrapped in a blanket sipping warm broth. Jael placed her head on Sarik's chest. She closed her eyes as the sound of his heartbeat lulled her to sleep.

For all the pain and exhaustion the day created, Sarik would have done it a thousand times over just to live in this moment again with Jael peacefully wrapped in his arms. The wind howled, blowing the heavy snowfall right though them. Sarik carried Jael into their tent and laid her down on the soft mattress left behind for them. He turned on the small heater in the corner of the tent and crawled under the covers. Sarik wrapped his arms and legs around Jael and produced whatever heat he could until he fell asleep.

By morning the entire tent was buried under the snow, and Sarik and Jael had to dig their way out. They spent much of the day uncovering and drying off their provisions, stuffing as much as they could in the tent. Sarik discovered much of the food rations had been pilfered by wild animals during the night.

"What do we have left?" she asked.

Thumbing through the box he said, "Mostly grains, all of the meat is gone."

Jael uncovered her bow and arrows from the snow. "Meat will not be a problem," she stated boldly, strapping the bow and quiver to her back. "I'll hunt while you finish organizing the camp.

"I'm not comfortable with you going out in the woods alone," he protested.

Furrowing her brow, Jael laughed. "I've been hunting since I was old enough to pull back a bow."

"I'm the one who should be hunting, not you." He puffed out his chest in a manly sort of way.

"You...hunt?" She let out a big belly laugh.

"I'm fully capable of killing things in the woods."

"Carful, Sarik, your ego is showing." She smiled.

Sarik smiled back at her and raised his brow. "Care to make a wager?"

"Alright, mister I-can-kill-things-in-the-woods, whatever each of us kills the other has to carry back to camp and dress," she proclaimed, sticking out her hand to shake on it.

He shook her hand and strapped his stunner to his hip. In less than an hour, Sarik found himself dragging a large elk through the woods and back to camp. "Did you have to kill the largest one you could find?" He grunted as he struggled. To add insult to injury, he had to admit to Jael that he had no idea how to dress an animal.

She pulled a standard issue knife out of one of the containers and tossed it to him. "I guess you're about to learn."

After watching him make a mess, she had enough pity to show him how to dress the elk.

"Okay, you win," he declared. "Just don't let word get out of my short comings. My manhood is at stake here." He laughed.

"Let it never be said, the great Prince Sarik was unmanned by the fair Lady Jael," she sassed. "Now get cooking! I'm famished."

Chapter 10

"Sarik, wake up," Jael whispered in his ear, shaking him lightly.

He rustled under the covers and his eyes cracked open. Jael put her finger over her lips and shushed him, then she pointed to the shadow just outside the tent door. Reaching for his stunner, Sarik strained to make out any discernible sound. Mentally he reached out to Jael, *"I hear voices,"* he projected into her mind. *"Don't talk with your voice. They might hear us, think what you want to say and direct it at me—like I'm doing."*

"Like this?"

Sarik nodded his head. *"Do you understand what they're saying?"*

"No, I don't know this language."

"How many?" he asked. Jael held up three fingers and Sarik nodded. *"We need to scare them off. Can you set the logs around the fire pit on fire from here?"*

Jael nodded.

"I'm going to make them see ghosts. When they start to get nervous set the logs on fire," he sent to her mind. She moved away from Sarik and positioned herself nearer to the target. He clasped her wrist holding her in place for a moment. She looked at him questioningly as he gave her a halfcocked grin. *"And make it big."*

Eyes closed, Sarik sat motionless in the middle of the tent. He concentrated on a ghostly image of demons and projected it into the robbers' minds. Jael felt fear well up inside of them as Sarik concentrated. As it peaked, she lit all of the logs and formed a massive inferno. Sarik created the image of a dragon out of the flames that chased the screaming bandits into the woods.

They let out a sigh and collapsed back down on the bed. "We're not safe here, and we still have two more days until the shuttle returns." Sarik reached over and pulled her closer.

Cuddling next to him with her head resting on his arm and neck, Jael considered what he said. "Surely they won't return, not after that scare." She placed her hand across his chest feeling safe in his arms.

"The problem is nobody else should be out here. This is an isolated area. M & E has been keeping tabs on the surrounding local populations and the nearest one is over seventy miles away. Plus, these men were on foot and didn't appear to be passing through." The wheels in his mind turned as he tried to figure out what they were doing in this area and who they were—their language wasn't one he was familiar with either.

"Since we're stuck out here for two more days, maybe we should investigate?" she said, excited for an adventure.

Squeezing her closer, he replied, "That might not be such a bad idea."

They dressed and readied their hiking gear. Sarik removed the binoculars and knife from the survey kit and loaded them into his pack along with a tiny two man tent. They packed their large tent and gear and hid them in the woods just outside of the camp, a precaution in case there were others nearby. He and Jael agreed they would follow the bandits until they had to return for the shuttle. Before they left camp, Sarik set their position on his nav-tracker and made one last look around.

It took hours to catch up with the men. Just as they expected, and to Sarik relief, there were only three of them who were dressed in furs and tunics of loosely woven wool. The tools they used to chop firewood were made of stone instead of metal, leading Sarik to believe they were a more primitive culture than the locals. After watching them in their camp for some time, Jael and Sarik continued their investigation. They hiked up and around the mountain to a river just on the other side. As they scanned the area, Jael noticed a crude, shallow draft boat on the bank. It was just large enough for the three men and their belongings, but not much more. The sun was setting, so they hiked further up the mountain and away from the river. Once they felt they were far enough away, they made camp.

The snow on the mountain was still high from the storm that passed through five days ago, so Sarik cleared an area for the tent and fire and Jael went to look for wood. By the time Jael returned, Sarik had finished setting up camp. Within minutes the fire was going, and their boots and socks were drying while their food cooked.

"What's your assessment of these people?" she asked.

"We've tracked similar tribes in the north, but I don't recall them getting around much." He poked at the fire with a stick. "It looks like they got here by boat and that they're alone. Do you recall your father mentioning encounters with these kinds of people?"

"The only ones I can think of are the Beakers, but they're nothing like the men we've been watching."

"They're definitely not Beakers. I guess M & E still have work to do before the Asgard and Valhalla get here." He stretched his legs in front of him then rolled his head from side to side to relax the muscles in his neck.

Getting up, Jael massaged Sarik's neck. When she got to an area of tension, she pressed firmly on the spot with her thumb and created heat until the tension melted away.

"How did you learn to do that?" he moaned.

Jael's warm hands still worked the muscles in his neck.

"The neck massage, I learned when I was young. Father would get headaches from the stress and this always helped. But since you taught me how to heat, it makes it much easier to loosen the muscles. Besides, I can feel where you're hurting like it's my own pain," she explained, continuing her massage.

"How very odd. I know the Jinn are telepathic, but I don't know any who are empathic."

"What is empathic?"

"Empathy is the ability to feel what another is feeling."

She stopped rubbing his neck and sat down beside him. "Well, it's only been the last couple of days that I've been able to feel what you're feeling, but it's getting stronger."

Putting his arm around her, he said, "I need to show you how to block that before you become overwhelmed with everyone else's emotions."

After dinner they went to bed. Jael lay there half-awake thinking about everything that happened and where her life was headed. There was much she didn't know about Sarik, but she wanted to. "What's it like to travel among the stars?"

"Unlike you, they're peacefully quiet," he teased.

"One day I'd like to see them." She sleepily yawned.

Sarik could imagine traveling the stars with Jael next him. "Jael, when you first got to Atlantis, I thought of you as nothing more than a contractual obligation. Then your beauty captivated me and all I could think of was having your body next to mine." He stared at the roof of the tent. "After spending time with you, I can see I made a big mistake. You're so much more than a pawn or a pretty face. You've managed to instill in me the one thing no one else could—humility." He paused for a moment, took a deep breath and let it out. "I can't believe I'm about to say this, but I love you." Sarik held her close and waited for a response. But none came. Jael softly snored in his ear, completely unaware of his confession.

~~

It was a long, mountainous hike back to their original camp. The shuttle arrived early, and the captain had remainder of their camp packed and loaded while they waited for Sarik and Jael to return. Just as the two came out of the woods, Captain Ross walked over to greet them. Before he could say anything, Sarik shot him a look that quashed any attempt at apologizing and continued to walk towards the shuttle.

"I was following orders," he yelled after Sarik before following them into the shuttle.

Exhausted, they slept the entire ride back to Hy-Brasil. When they reached Sarik's quarters, they were surprised to find Varen and Salima waiting for them.

"Couldn't you two have at least waited until we had a chance to take a hot shower and eat a decent meal?" Sarik threw his bags down by the front door.

"No. A messenger has just arrived from Eir with news for you two. Jael, please sit," Varen said sternly as he waited for her to comply before he continued.

Judging by the look on Salima's face, Jael knew the news could not be good. She sat on one of the couches in the living room, and Sarik joined her, holding her hand.

"Your father has been killed. He passed yesterday. Poisoning is suspected." Varen relayed what the messenger said. "I've sent a shuttle to retrieve his body, and it should arrive shortly."

Jael's face went completely white as she squeezed hard on Sarik's hand then started to sob. Sarik wrapped his arms around her, allowing her to cry into his chest. When her tears subsided, he released her.

Looking into her red swollen eyes, Sarik held her hands. "I'm sorry, Jael," he said as a single tear rolled down his face in memory of his friend.

Fisting her hand, Jael asked through gritted teeth, "Who did this?"

"The envoy I've sent is trying to determine that as we speak before Dugun makes them leave, but I'm afraid it will be left to your clan to get to the bottom of things." replied Varen.

"Dugun and Wren were there early for your wedding, as well as Betta and Haro. Tam and Lenni were in Dunfin, but they're expected home in two days. Jael, your father has designated Sarik as heir, but that was pending your marriage. Before your father's body was even cold, Dugun pronounced himself Laird," explained Salima.

"Dugun has already stopped all trade with Hy-Brasil and is preventing our people from helping find your father's killer," Varen added.

Jael's head was spinning. Her father was dead and nothing was going as he planned. She looked in to Sarik's eyes and knew what she had to do. "Sarik—" was all she got out before she started to cry again.

He held her in his arms. "I'll have our marriage papers ready to be signed within the hour," he said, before she could ask.

"No need. I took the liberty of doing that already. You just need to sign them in front of a legal clerk, and I can have one of those here in less than five minutes." Varen pulled out papers from a folder on the end table and called for a clerk.

"I'll arrange for a shuttle to take you to Eir tomorrow evening. I fear for your safety, Jael, so Var, Tal, and I will accompany you. Dugun will not keep the priestesses from their job of comforting the people," said Salima.

A few minutes later, the clerk was at the front door. Jael nervously signed the papers, then Sarik signed with his hands shaking uncontrollably. Varen smiled and shook Sarik's hand then gave Jael a hug. "Welcome to the family," he said before he left with Salima.

Grabbing two glasses, Sarik poured himself and Jael a drink. They sat next to each other on the couch not knowing what to say. After the first sip, Jael inhaled deeply and crinkled her nose, waving her hand in front of it. "Gods, you stink!" she exclaimed.

"Well you don't smell much better." He laughed. "I have an idea. How about a quick shower then a nice, long, hot soak?" He took a sip of his drink and watched her reaction.

"Aren't you worried I might drown?" she asked.

"No, because I'll be there to keep that from happening." He gave her a halfcocked smile and raised is brow.

Jael took another sip of her drink. "Whatever this drink is, it's divine," she said, attempting to steer the conversation in a different direction.

"It's Cerulean Ale. What are you afraid of?"

"Sarik, everything has happened so fast. It scares me," Jael swallowed hard as her eyes teared.

"Do I scare you?"

"No, that's not what I meant."

"Oh. So touching me scares you. Well that's a bit awkward since you just spent the last two weeks in my bed." He laughed to break the tension.

"Yes, but that was only to stay warm," she poked back.

"Ouch, not even married for ten minutes, and already you've wounded me," he replied and placed his hands over his heart. "I know exactly what you mean. And you don't have to worry; you can have as much time as you need. If I had almost drowned, I'd be scared of the bathtub too."

All joking aside, Jael placed her hand on Sarik's knee. "Sarik, you know you didn't have to marry me," she said, seriously.

"But I wanted to." Drinking the rest of his ale, he stood and reached for Jael's hand then led her to the bathroom.

~~

The shuttle landed in an isolated area just passed Halis and Edric's cottage. Halis waited for them with horses ready for the ride to Halor. Jael tugged at the fabric of her gown. It had been nearly a month since she'd worn it, and she forgot how uncomfortable it was compared to the clothes in Atlantis. But she had to admit, Sarik looked more handsome than ever in the black, metal studded tunic and form fitting leather trousers. He had the appearance of a divine conqueror. The moment he put them on a stern, business-like attitude replaced his usual playfulness as if the clothes made the man.

Before they reached Halor, the party was intercepted by Kale and Jaren. "Dugun's men have already taken over the estate. I recommend you stay with me for tonight. He's throwing himself a banquet tomorrow, and it'll be safer to pay your respects then," Kale advised.

Sarik let out a deep exhale. "So, Dugun wants to do things the hard way. Very well then, tonight we'll come up with a plan to end this swiftly before Dugun gets too comfortable. When do you expect Tam?"

"He and the others should be home before the banquet, providing their escorts don't slow them down," replied Kale.

"Whose men escort them?" asked Jael.

"I sent your father's guard captain Fairen, plus a couple of guards to retrieve them. Ugis and Edric are with them also. I worry for their safety after the attempt on Tam and Lenni's lives on their way to Blackrock."

"Why was I not informed about this attempt on their lives?" She glared at Kale.

Kale sat up straight and raised his brow at Jael's commanding demeanor. "When we got word of it, you were unavailable."

Sarik glanced back at the priestesses. "That's not going to be enough protection this time, Kale. It's obvious Dugun wants them dead, and now that he has made himself laird, his men will stop at nothing to see to that they are. I'll send Tal to Harwell to escort them the rest of the way." He motioned for Tal to catch up with them and told her their plan. She turned her stag pony around and headed back to the shuttle.

"I'd love to see the look on their faces when Dugun's men find out they're dealing with a female Jinn," Kale said and chuckled. "Thank you for sending her, Sarik. I should like to have Tam and Ugis home in one piece."

"How many men did Dugun come with?" Jael asked.

Jaren piped in, "He has about twenty at the house and another forty or so in the surrounding woods. Plus he has an army of about two to three hundred on the border at Annoc."

"I hadn't anticipated an army that large. This may take more time than I hoped," Sarik said to Jael and frowned.

"Kale, how many men do you have who will support me and Sarik with Tam as our council?"

"Maybe eighty or so here, but given time we could raise an army big enough to defeat Canulis itself," assured Kale.

"If anything were to happen to Laird Canulis, that's precisely what we'll have to do," Sarik shook his head.

Jael listened as Sarik continued the conversation of war with Kale, she now understood the reason her father had picked Sarik as her husband and his heir. He was the only one able to deliver her people from Dugun's hands and still allow her to rule as her father wanted.

At Kale's home they were welcomed by his wife Fe. They sat at the dining table and devised a plan to rid Eir of Dugun. Var kept company with Fe, whose nerves were frayed from the thought of her sons' impending danger. After a couple of hours of disputing, Sarik pounded his fist on the table.

"Jael, you can't captain an army, you need to learn how to use your gifts. We're going to need as much psychokinetic power as we can get and it's time you learn to be who you really are. Salima is going to spend the next few days teaching you the basics. After that Tal will teach you how to use your powers to win in battle." Sarik threw his hands up in the air and walked away from the table.

Jael followed him with her eyes. "Why can't we use the resources of Atlantis?"

"We have higher directives. One of which is to not involve ourselves in human conflict and to live in anonymity while here. If not for our marriage, I wouldn't be allowed to get involved without breaking rules, which could get me imprisoned or even a death sentence. That's why your father asked for our betrothal and not just for help securing his lands," Sarik explained.

"And what of Salima, Tal and Var? Do they not break the rules?"

"Not when it comes down to helping other Jinn; even though technically, Var is Nauss and not Jinn—she belongs to the same protectorate," Salima told her. "Even if you had not married Sarik, you still would have fallen in our jurisdiction of protection. The only problem is unlike Sarik, we are not great tacticians—it is something he is gifted with."

Jael looked at Sarik and waited for his ego to rear its ugly head. Instead, he seemed humbled by Salima's comment. There was much she had to learn and most of it would be not about being a Jinn, but rather the enigma that was her husband. "What's our plan for tomorrow?"

Sarik sat back in his chair. "Tomorrow we quietly disable the guards in the woods and then we attend the banquet as guests of the new laird. We need to assess the situation from the inside before acting." He put his fingers on his chin and had a faraway look in his eyes.

"What's wrong?" Jael asked.

"I find it odd Haro has not protested any of this. I wonder if he has sided with Dugun?" he thought aloud.

Kale furrowed his brow. "Now that you mention it, I've noticed his unusual behavior too. I think we should keep an eye on him. I don't know him well enough to say whether I trust him or not."

Remembering back, Jael chimed in, "I know Lenni spent some time with Haro and Betta, maybe she'll have some insight as to whether he can be trusted. As far as my own encounters with him, he seems to lack in the intelligence department."

"I wish Tam were here already. I needed for the clan to know we have his support." Sarik sighed, leaning back in his chair.

"I've taken care of most of that already. As soon as we heard of Jael's marriage, the clan agreed you should rule with Tam as your council. It's just a matter of removing Dugun without bloodshed." Kale shrugged his shoulders. "Besides, as long as Dugun believes no one challenges his claim, we can take him by surprise."

Arms laden with hot bowls, Fe walked over to the table and sat them down in front of everyone. "I'm sorry. All I have is yesterday's stew. I was told you would dine with us only moments after your arrival, otherwise I would have prepared meat," she explained as she retrieved a basket of rolls.

"Please don't apologize. Your stew is delicious, and we are thankful you have provided it for us," Sarik responded, spooning the stew into his mouth.

Jael took one bite and savored it in her mouth. "Mmm...I forgot how much I missed your cooking, Fe." Reaching for a roll, she sensed Sarik's desire for one, so she grabbed two and passed one to him.

Kale laid his wooden spoon across his bowl and suggested, "We should take the shuttle out in the morning and get a better count of Dugun's army on the border."

"Why don't you and Jaren do that while I help Salima train Jael?" proposed Sarik, soaking a piece of roll in his stew then eating it.

Quick to reply, Jaren jeered, "There's no way I'm going to ride in the belly of the dragon again, not after what happen last time." He crossed his arms in front of him in defiance.

"Jaren, it's normal for one to lose their breakfast when the weather is rough outside." Sarik laughed at the cross look Jaren gave him.

"I'm not doing it. No matter how hard you try to convince me." He pursed his lips tightly.

"Very well, I concede. However, Captain Ross will be sad not to see you again, especially after the mess you left for him last time."

"If you don't mind, I would like to take Var with me. She could be useful as far as picking up the soldiers' thoughts. It might give us some idea of what they have planned," requested Kale.

"Excellent idea. Var, if you don't mind the telepathic intrusion, could you accompany Kale tomorrow?" he asked, looking towards her.

"Under normal circumstances I would protest, but to prevent deaths, I'm willing to bend that rule," she replied.

"What rule?" Jael was confused by their conversation.

"When you live in a telepathic society there are rules, or should I say, common courtesies that we follow—such as not invading other people's thoughts without their permission. It keeps us civil," he explained.

"Oh...that makes complete sense." After thinking about it for a few seconds, Jael blushed, realizing she had been intruding on Sarik's thoughts quite often.

"Sarik, I'm so sorry. I had no idea there were rules against reading your thoughts," apologized Jael.

"Jael, the only thoughts of mine you've read are the ones I have allowed you to. So, don't apologize, you've done nothing wrong." Sarik clasped her hand and grinned.

Relieved she wasn't breaking the rules, Jael relaxed and finished her stew. She waited for Sarik to finish then they excused themselves for the night. It had been a long and emotional day, and Jael was haggard from stress and lack of sleep. She changed into her night shift and let out a sigh. Sarik wrapped his arms around her waist. "How are you holding up?"

"I've been better." She closed her eyes and enjoyed his embrace.

"You look worn and it worries me," he said, kissing the top of her head.

She turned around in his arms to face him. "As long as you're with me, I'll be fine."

He bent down and kissed her softly on the lips before picking her up and laying her on the bed. Once next to her, exhaustion took over, and he swiftly fell asleep.

C.G. Powell   130

Chapter 11

Shortly after sundown, the road weary group arrived at the inn in Harwell. Tam greeted the innkeeper and discussed sleeping arrangements for the night. They were interrupted by a tall, beautiful woman with dark hair. It was evident from her long blue robe and gem incrusted scimitar that she was a priestess from Hy-Brasil.

She gave a slight bow to Tam. "I'm Tal. Sarik has sent me to escort your party the remainder of the way." She reached into a small pouch at her hip and pulled out a small, folded note. "Your father sent this."

Tam opened the note and read:

You and your brother are in the best hands I could leave you in.

I anxiously await your safe return.

Kale

Before Tam could speak to his new guard, she rushed to the door to greet Fairen.

"Fairen!" Tal beamed and threw her arms around his neck.

He put his arms around her waist and pulled her against his chest before passionately kissing her lips. "Talia, my love, what brings you here?"

Fairen looked old enough to be Tal's father. Tam raised his brow then cleared his throat. "I take it you two know each other."

Fairen coughed, glanced down, and rubbed the back of his neck. "You could say that."

Tal laughed at Fairen's embarrassment then firmly placed her hand on his backside. "I like the way he carries his sword."

Grasping his stomach, Tam let out a big belly laugh. He'd never seen Fairen shaken by anything, but this woman clearly knew how to get the best of him.

"What are you laughing at? I've seen the way you look at Lady Lenni, and had she been a common wench, you would be more public with your affections," he retorted.

Tam's laugh faded to a whisper. "Is it that obvious?"

"Is what obvious?" Lenni whispered from behind Tam.

Tam jumped then turned to face Lenni. She looked at him with a halfcocked grin.

"Summer can't come quick enough." Tam wrapped his arms around her waist and kissed her.

~~

Sore from the previous day's ride, Lenni spent the whole morning grumbling. Their swift pace right from the start had certainly not helped her already foul disposition, save for the fact that she would be home soon. "Can we stop soon? This pace is exhausting," complained Lenni.

"There's a river not far from here. We'll stop when we get there so the horses can rest and drink too," said Fairen, who was riding between Lenni and Tam. He turned his head and noticed Tal craning her neck as if to hone in on something, so he fell back to talk with her.

"We're being followed. I'll need someone to take my horse and belongings so I can track our stalker," she said to Fairen.

"Tam, take Lenni and others to the river post haste," commanded Fairen then replied to Tam's concerned look. "I'll meet you there shortly. Now get going."

Tam and the others galloped away. As soon as the party was out of sight, Tal got off her horse and handed the reins to Fairen. Her skin turned an odd hue of blue while she untied her robe and let it fall to the ground. Fairen closed his eyes and looked away out of respect as she stuffed her clothes in her bag. She stood in the forest naked; her mind reached out to a nearby pack of wolves. While she waited for the pack, her body changed to match theirs—except her catlike eyes glowed an eerie green.

Hearing the growls of nearby wolves, Fairen opened his eyes and looked down, completely unfazed by her wolf form. "I'll meet you at the river." He turned his horse around and headed to join Tam with Tal's horse in tow.

Tal's wolf nodded then joined the rest of the pack to hunt down their prey. They swiftly found their target and surrounded him in a small open area of the woods. As he drew his bow, Tal set fire to it in the shape of a snake climbing up to his hand. He dropped his bow and screamed, then ran through the only gap the wolves left open—part of Tal's well-orchestrated plan. He sprinted through the bushes and between low branches while the wolves herded him toward the river where Fairen and his men waited for their unarmed victim.

The man was out of breath and confused when he finally made it the river. Before he had time to process what was going on, Ugis tackled him to the ground. Tam tied up their captive while Fairen walked into the forest with Tal's clothes and left them in a well-covered area for her. Soon Tal joined them, her flesh back to its human color, without any trace of the wolf she had been just moments before. She walked up to their prisoner with Fairen. Her eyes glowed green while she stared into his.

"Who do you ssserve?" she said slowly, hissing the last word as a snake would as she set her truth charm.

The scared man shook, trying his best to resist her question. "Dugun of Canulis," he stammered uncontrollably.

"What are your orderssss?" she crooned in the man's ear.

"To kill Tam and the Lady Lenni of Eir," he cried out in pain as he struggled to keep his secret.

"How many men are there?" she continued, her demeanor was more relaxed.

"Sixteen, including myself," he whispered, hanging his head down in shame.

One side of Tal's mouth curled up in a sadistic snarl. Satisfied that she had the answers she needed, she walked away and joined the others at the water's edge. She cleared the rocks from a sandy spot on the bank and motioned Tam and Fairen to join her where she sat on the ground, her legs crisscrossed like a child. Using a small twig she drew out a plan in the sand. Although it would be easy for her to consume their enemy in flames, she couldn't morally bring herself to do it. So, she came up with a plan to minimize casualties on both sides. To divide and conquer was her plan. She'd draw the enemy out in small groups then Fairen and the others would capture those she lured into her trap.

As Tal neared the camp of Dugun's men, she guised herself as a young girl. A childlike laughter echoed through the woods like a dryad drawing the men's attention. She peeped around one of the nearby trees and laughed again. Two of the men got up from the fire and followed her through the forest. When she lured them far enough away she changed into a mist that completely encompassed them, giving Fairen a chance to unarm and capture them.

When the first two men failed to return, their leader sent five more to find them. The fog rolled unnaturally towards them. Not knowing whether to continue through it or to run away, they stood there confused. As it got closer, the mist turned into an ominous black mass and climbed above them like a great hand reaching out. The men screamed in terror, dropping their weapons and clamoring to get away. Just as before, Fairen and the others were there to subdue them.

Now that the odds were more even, they moved to take the camp. Back in her human form, Tal entered the enemy's small camp. Their commander yelled for her to halt, but she continued to walk until she reached the edge of the fire. His men all had weapons pointed at her, awaiting his order to engage. Fog rolled in behind her, red glowing eyes penetrated the mist as they drew closer. A growl split the night like a demon ripped from the bowels of hell and doused them in ice-cold fear. Without command, one of the men let loose his arrow, but before it could hit its target it burst into flames and turned to ash that drifted on the wind, ending all hope of negotiating surrender. Not waiting for another to fly, Fairen and the others attacked.

Tal, once again, took her wolf form and joined the other wolves as they tore into the flesh of the enemy. When the battle was over, none of Dugun's men from the camp were left standing.

Tam was sickened by wolves ripping the flesh from the dead bodies. He was glad Lenni was in a safe area and away from the carnage. When he attempted to stop them, Tal stepped in.

"It's winter and the wolves need sustenance too. They must eat what they can to survive. To keep them from feeding to satisfy your own conscience is as inhuman as starving your own children. They're living things too."

Against all they had been taught, they left the bodies in the woods to be consumed by the wolves as Tal wished. When they got to where Lenni, Ugis, and Edric were watching the prisoners, Fairen realized it would take them too long to get home if they had to bring the prisoners on foot, so he and Tal stayed back to transport them as the rest rode ahead.

~~

Evening was already upon them when Sarik and Jael arrived at the banquet. The great hall was filled with members of the clan and a dozen or so of Dugun's men. Jael greeted Wren and Halis in the doorway, but to her surprise Betta and Haro were not there. Everyone sat down for the meal. Dugun, Wren, and two of Dugun's guards sat at the table on the raised platform, completely overlooking the fact Sarik was a prince in his own right and should have been given a place of honor on the dais. Unaffected by Dugun's intended insult, Sarik and Jael sat with Kale and Fe at the far end of the room.

The hall was quiet save the grumbled whispers of a few of its occupants, but half way through the meal, the doors to the great hall flew open. Tam entered the room and treaded his way to the dais. Sarik stood to intercept him, but he was too late.

"How dare you put a price on my head, Dugun?" Tam accused through clinched teeth, stepping up on the platform, hands fisted as if ready to fight.

Before Tam could say another word, Dugun's guards grabbed him by the arms. Tam fought to get out of their grasp, but before he could get free, Dugun stabbed him in the stomach with his sword. He pulled his sword out of Tam's gut and positioned himself to strike again, but Sarik had already run across the room and jumped over the table on the dais. His hand clasped around Dugun's throat and the other caught the wrist of the hand holding the sword. Sarik's grip was like fire against Dugun's wrist. Electricity coursed through it like a storm and caused Dugun to drop his weapon. Lenni's screams could be heard in the background as Salima rushed past her to where Tam lay crumpled on the dais.

Clansmen disarmed the guards who held Tam and the other ones in the room. Through gritted teeth, Sarik growled, "Dugun, if you value your life, you and your men will leave and never show yourself here again." Sarik put Dugun back on the ground and stormed after Salima and Var. Jaren stepped in to ensure that all of Dugun's men were removed from the estate. Jael and Halis begged for Wren to stay, but she followed Dugun instead.

Sarik dashed down the hall on Salima's heels. Once inside Rowe's private chamber, he threw the door closed and asked, "How's he doing?"

Salima looked up, her dress covered in Tam's blood. "He is losing a lot of blood. You and Var need to stop the bleeding, and I'll stop his pain."

Var sat on the floor with Tam's head in her lap. She and Sarik placed their hands over his wound and mentally stitched it back together cell by cell from the inside out. Salima kept eye contact with him and mentally stopped his pain so he would stay still.

When they were done, Sarik sighed, "I hope he hasn't lost too much blood."

Salima moved away from Tam's side. "I'm no healer, Sarik. I could serve you better if I helped Jaren gather Dugun's men," she said.

"Go ahead, but only the men on the grounds. Tell Jaren we'll clear the forest in the morning," he commanded, getting up from the floor and sitting in the large chair behind the table.

"He needs fluids. I'll get him some water," Var volunteered just as Kale threw the door open.

"How is he?" Kale asked, his face white as a sheet. Walking to where Tam's listless body was lying on the floor, he bent down next to him. Kale brushed the hair from his son's eyes.

"It looks like he'll be alright, but he has lost a lot of blood," replied Sarik.

Kale let out a sigh of relief then clasped Tam's hand. "Lenni is worried out of her mind right now. I thought you should know," he said to Tam, not knowing if he was asleep or awake.

"Can I see her?" Tam moaned.

Kale smiled. "Yes, I'll let her in. She paces in front of the door as we speak." He got up and opened the door to find Lenni's face pressed against it.

Pushing Kale aside, she rushed to where Tam was and held his hand. "You had me so worried. I thought you were dead when they carried you out of the great hall," she sobbed.

"We need to clean him up and get him off the floor," Sarik said from his chair.

When Lenni looked up to see who was speaking, her face went completely white. Before her was the man who haunted her dreams. *Who was he, and why was he here?* she asked herself as the blood rushed back to her face.

Standing and extending his hand to greet her, he introduced himself. "You must be Lenni? I'm Sarik, Jael's husband." He kissed her hand before sitting back down in his chair.

Lenni's heart sank as she realized the man of her dreams was her sister's husband. All of the time she spent looking for him was for nothing. She felt Tam stir and realized she was finally free to follow what her heart had been telling her all along.

"Yes, I'm Lenni. Thank you for saving his life." She turned her gaze back Tam's pale face and placed her hand on his cheeks. "I found my mystery man, and he's not at all the person I believed him to be," she whispered in his ear and laughed softly between stifled sobs.

Tam put his hand around the back of her neck and turned his head to face her. He smiled, pulling her closer, and kissed her lips softly before closing his eyes and drifting into unconsciousness. Tears quietly streamed down Lenni's face. She gently placed her hand on his chest and rested her head on his shoulders.

Sarik and Var gave Lenni a few minutes before they moved Tam to the laird's bed chamber to recuperate. After a brief visit, Kale and Ugis left Tam in Lenni's hands and headed to the great hall where Sarik, Var, and a few of the prominent clansmen were talking. The hall was emptied of its guest and the banquet cleared from the tables. Their argument was loud and heated until Kale stepped into the hall with Ugis behind him. Silence filled the great room as all heads turned to them.

"How does Tam fair?" asked one of the men.

Kale let out a deep breath before responding. "He does well and should be back on his feet in no time."

Everyone breathed a sigh of relief before continuing their discussion. Soon Tal and Fairen arrived with their prisoners and joined the others in the great hall. "Fairen, I'll need you and Tal to help Jaren clear the forest of Dugun's men tomorrow," commanded Sarik. "Kale, we're going to need an army, and I'm willing to spare no cost."

"Sarik, there's still a problem with this plan," said Kale.

Sarik raised a curious brow. "What might that be?"

"Your marriage to Jael. You are not married until you do it before the clan. As far as they can see, you're just betrothed," Kale replied.

"Are you telling me our marriage in Hy-Brasil is not being recognized by the clan? If so, then why in God's name have I taken the laird's estate from its rightful heir according to your clan law?" His voice resonated throughout the hall in utter irritation.

"Settle down, Sarik. The clan will recognize you as heir as soon as you wed Jael in front of them—and provide a wedding feast," Kale smirked.

Letting out an exasperated breath, Sarik replied, "This is absolute madness, Kale. Please tell me you jest."

"No, Sarik, the clan has spoken and that is their demand before things go any further."

"I see," he said. After a moment he sneered. "Then you better find the clan elder and have him here before Jaren returns with the clansmen," he directed Kale. "Var, fetch Lady Jael. She's in town trying to calm everyone. See to it she is dressed and ready within the hour." Pausing only for a second, he looked to the stunned gaggle of clansmen before him and added, "I suggest you get going if you plan on having everyone here before we feast." As soon as he was done barking orders, he turned on his heel and stormed out of the hall.

Tal was quick to catch up with him in the hallway. "And what of your feast?" she asked, causing Sarik to stop dead in his tracks.

He rolled his eyes and turned back to look at her. "Since my father was so quick to wed me into this clan of crazies, call him and tell him I desire a wedding feast deserving of a god, and I want it here before midnight." He continued his quickened pace to the laird's bedroom to check on Tam before he completely lost his temper.

When he walked into the room, Tam was sitting up in bed talking to Lenni, some of his color had returned which was a good sign. "Well, you're looking better." He walked over to the bed.

"I'm feeling much better, thank you," Tam replied. "I know we've not been properly introduced, but I assume you are Jael's husband Sarik."

"That I am. Well, sort of," Sarik added. Skirting around his vague introduction, Sarik sputtered, "Glad you're feeling better because you have a wedding to attend in a couple of hours, and you're standing up with me."

"Are you and Jael not wed already?" he asked, confused by Sarik's request.

"We were married in Atlantis, but your clan is being stubborn and insists we are not wed until we are wed before them."

Lenni and Tam looked at each other and smiled. "Sarik, would it bother you if Lenni and I were wed at your ceremony too?"

"I think that would be a splendid idea. I could use a brother to save me from this clan's lunacy." He chuckled.

"Don't be so hard on them. It's not every day they get to attend a prince's wedding. It would be a shame to deny them their celebration," said Tam.

"It's not the celebration that bothers me as much as the timing. Dugun and his men are still a very much a threat, and instead of making ready for war, they request a wedding," Sarik complained, sitting on the foot of the bed.

"I can't say I blame them. They haven't had much to be happy about lately, especially with Rowe's death only a few days ago."

Before Sarik had a chance to reply, the door swung open and an irate Jael entered. "What is this nonsense all about, Sarik?"

"Your clan is refusing to follow my orders until we are wed before them," he stated bluntly.

"But we are already wed," she argued, before sitting on the foot of the bed next to Sarik.

"Apparently we're not wed until they say we're wed, but look on the bright side, Jael, Tam and Lenni are going to get married tonight too. At least their union will not be a celebratory farce like ours."

"Couldn't this have waited until we're done dealing with Dugun and laid my father to rest?" she said, before fully comprehended Sarik's remarks. Pausing for a second, she turned to Lenni and Tam. "You two are getting married?" She eyed the couple while she waited for their response.

Tam and Lenni looked at each other and smiled, before Lenni answered. "Yes."

Jael's agitation melted as she ran to Lenni and threw her arms around her neck. She clasped Tam's hand, bent over, and kissed his cheek. "Now you really are going to be my brother." She laughed.

"And you're still going to be the sister I never wanted," he teased and the room erupted in laughter.

～～

Jael stood on the dais next to Sarik. Unlike the quick and unceremonious signing of papers in Atlantis, this wedding felt real. For all of her admiration, Jael still knew little of her husband and even less about wifely duties. She was thankful Sarik had not pressed the issue yet, but how much more would he be able to stand before seeking comfort elsewhere as per their contract? She gazed over at Sarik. It was hard to believe such a man could be her husband. She became lost in his blue eyes—like watching the sea after a storm. *"Jael....Jael. The ceremony is over. Are you just going to stand there staring at me or kiss me?"* He intruded in her mind, startling her back to the present.

Sarik leaned over and kissed her quickly on the lips before she could reply, a response to the awkward silence of the clan as they waited for them to kiss. Tam and Lenni were also waiting before they locked lips in a more passionate kiss. "Are you okay?" asked Sarik as worry crossed his brow in the din of clapping and cheering.

"I'm fine. Just a little lost in thought." she replied in a whisper.

The crowd that gathered in the hall cheered louder as the couples turned to face them after their kisses. Soon the food was brought to the tables, it was a feast unlike any they had ever seen: soups, breads, cheeses and meats filled every table. In the back of the room sat the most extraordinary cake. It was five layers covered in a strange confection called icing that beautifully decorated it. Sarik's father had sent a message with the feast.

My dearest son,

Please enjoy the food. If I had known a feast was all you required to get you to settle down, I would have thrown you one a couple hundred years ago. Congratulations again on your nuptials, and I look forward to the grandchildren you two shall give me.

Best wishes,

Varen Alexander Sarik Poseidon

Lord of house Tintagel, King of Hy-Brasil, Captain of the Atlantis

Chapter 12

Dugun rode hard for two days. Upon his arrival at the camp in Annoc, he immediately walked into the main tent without greeting any of his men. At the far end of the tent in a large ornate chair behind a table, a man who appeared to be no older than Dugan sat. He pursed his lips and tapped on the table at Dugun's unexpected arrival. Dugun nervously walked towards the man, knowing he was the source of the man's agitation, and sat in the chair across from him.

The man cleared his throat. "Dugun, you're such an idiot. Your orders were simple: secure the Laird of Eir's estate until your father is taken care of. Then you'd have full command of his army. Now, I have an even bigger problem on my hands. Not only is Tam still alive, but your actions have turned the entire clan against you."

"He shouldn't have made it out of the forest. How was I to know the prince of Hy-Brasil would bring those witches with him? This is not turning out as you planned, and even with my father's army, I don't know if we can win," Dugun stated defensively.

"Did you find the papers I sent you for?" the stoic figure asked, ignoring Dugun's rant.

"I found the hidden papers, but I can't read them," he said. Pulling the papers out of his bag, he handed them over.

The man looked over them then smiled. "We have everything we need to remove Sarik as laird. All of our answers lie at the henge in Nesgrane, but we need to get there before Rowe's funeral precession in five days," he said, flames flashing across his eyes like a demon straight out of hell. "Take a handful of men and the fastest horses to the henge. This map shows the location of a box that Rowe buried there. I want the box here in no more than seven days. And, Dugun, don't screw this up."

Grabbing the map from the table, Dugun turned and left the tent. He selected a couple of trusted men and fresh horses then began his journey, making sure to stay within the borders of Canulis. If all went as planned, he would return from Nesgrane the new laird of Canulis—his older brother died in a hunting accident recently and left no children to make a claim. Once his father was dead, it all would be his. Somewhere in the back of Dugun's mind a voice yelled out in protest. The loss of his brother was a sad affair, but necessary for his plan. Seconds from stopping in his tracks and protesting the killing of his father, Dugun's mind pulled away from the loving thoughts of his dad and settled on the power he would gain.

~~

It took two days to clear the forest of Dugun's men. By the time everyone returned to Halor, the precession to the burial henge at Nesgrane was ready to begin. Rowe's body had been prepared for burial. They concluded in Atlantis that he was killed by hemlock, a plant that grew wild in the woods and was accessible to everyone. Just as Mila's had been, Rowe's body would be brought to the henge by the priesthood the day of the burial.

Sarik adapted easily into the role of laird. His confidence and ability to make a well thought out decisions gave the clan comfort during their time of great uncertainty. Unfortunately, this persona was a different than the one Jael had fallen in love with in Atlantis. This Sarik was all business; each action was cold and calculated, and every moment was consumed with clan issues, which left Jael feeling like an outsider around her husband—even in private.

In the laird's chamber that she and Sarik shared, Jael put the last of her things in her saddlebag as Sarik walked in.

"Are you almost ready?" he asked.

She closed the flap of the bag and paused for a second. As he walked over to grab the bag from Jael, she looked straight at him. "Do you love me, Sarik?"

The seriousness melted from his face as he took the bag from her hand and threw it back on the bed. He placed his arms around her waist and drew her closer, gently kissing her lips. Eyes closed and his forehead resting on hers, he whispered, "I'm sorry, Jael. I didn't mean to overlook you these last few days." He released her from his embrace.

Tears welled in her eyes, threatening to stain her face.

"I've been so occupied with protecting the clan's interest I've ignored the entire reason why I'm doing this. It's *because* I love you, Jael, and I don't want to let you or your clan down. I promise as soon as things are settled we can go back to Atlantis and just be Jael and Sarik without the pressures of being Laird and Lady of Eir."

Jael took a deep breath and let it out. "I didn't mean to be needy. As soon as we got here, it was like you were a completely different person. Not that I don't admire your strength and character, I just miss the Sarik I fell in love with in Atlantis."

"Don't you mean the Sarik you unmanned in the woods while we were stranded?" He laughed.

Smiling, her mood lightened as she thought back to the week in the woods. "Yes, I miss that poor misguided fellow."

Grabbing her bag, he gave her one last embrace and kiss before they left the room together. Out in the courtyard the rest of the clan gathered. It was later than Sarik wanted to leave as the slow precession was already going to take five days—six if they didn't leave soon. When the last of the clan arrived, they began the long trip to the henge. Sarik and Tam rode at the head with Kale behind them and Jaren in the rear with the Var and Tal, for protection. Earlier that morning, Sarik ordered a shuttle to secretly fly over the area they would pass and make sure it was clear of Dugun's men or bandits. Assured that the forest was clear, they made their way into the woods. The pace was slow; most of the clan's members were on foot, so Tam and Sarik rode ahead and found areas to rest. As the sun set, Sarik and the rest of the men on horseback rode to an area he and Tam scouted earlier to set up the tents and made camp.

As the clan settled in for the night, Sarik and Jael made their way around the camp to ensure everyone's comfort. When they finished, Sarik placed his hands over Jael's eyes and walked her to an area right outside of where the rest of the clan was located.

"Where are you taking me?" She laughed, curious as to what he was up to.

"It's a surprise," he teased, before stopping and removing his hands.

Before her was the camp where she and Sarik stayed on their M & E trip. She smiled and threw her arms around him.

"I had the shuttle drop it off on their last fly by. I miss being as close as we were on those cold nights and thought we could use a little time to ourselves," he said.

She kissed him on the cheek before entering the tent. "It's more than I could have asked for."

Soon they were curled in each other's arms and as Jael started to get comfortable, Sarik smiled. "There's only one thing left for us to do to make this marriage binding," he pointed out, turning the lights down low.

She clasped his hand and looked into his eyes. "I'm scared," she whispered.

Moving the wisps of hair from her face, he smiled. "What are you afraid of?"

"What if it hurts or I don't know what I'm doing and hurt you?" she confessed, looking away.

He ran his fingers down her cheek, pulling her back into his gaze. "Jael, you're not going to hurt me." He softly laughed, kissing her lightly down her jawline until he reached her lips where he kissed her with all the raw passion of a man lusting after his wife. He pulled her closer and whispered in her ear, "I want to share with you what it will be like." He leaned his forehead against hers.

Opening her mind fully to him, she felt a slight pressure building inside of her. It moved through her until its fullness reached her womb, causing her to squirm and take in a big breath. He let go of the mental connection and waited for her to exhale. "That's what it is going to feel like, Jael," he said, his fingers lightly running down her back, making her to shiver.

"And what of the pain?" she asked.

"It only hurts for a minute, and I can block that for you. After that you'll want to feel everything."

"If it feels anything like what you showed me, then yes, I'll want to feel everything." She chuckled nervously.

"We'll take things nice and slow." He stood and removed his clothes.

Jael stared at him; the dim light accentuated every well-formed muscle in his body and left her breathless. She swallowed hard and grabbed hold of his out stretched hand, beckoning for her to join him. He loosened the drawstring at the top of her shift, and let it fall to her shoulders before kissing her lips. She pulled him closer and ran her fingers down his muscular back, stopping just shy of his rear.

He let out a moan, withdrawing his lips from hers. His tongue moved down her neck, leaving a trail of butterfly kisses all the way to the top of her now bare chest. On his knees, he cupped her breast with one hand while the other rested on the small of her back, keeping her close to him. Moving his tongue in circles around her nipple, he stopped just long enough to blow cold air across it so it would stand up, then he placed the pert tip between his lips, drawing it into his mouth. Jael moaned. Gabbing hold of his hair with both hands, her knees went weak. He scooped her into his arms and laid her on the bed.

Her beautiful nakedness before him made a halfcocked grin creep onto his handsome face before he picked up where he left off. She put her hand on his chest and gently pushed him away to get his attention.

"What's wrong?" he asked, stopping everything.

She paused then let out a sigh. "I don't know what I'm supposed to be doing," she admitted, biting her plump lower lip.

Leaning back on his elbow, he touched her cheek. "Jael, my love, do whatever pleases you. Kiss, touch, rub, taste whatever you like. Do what feels good and don't be afraid to explore. Open your mind, Jael. I want to know what gives you pleasure." He moved his hand to her breast and rolled her nipple between his thumb and index finger. "I can feel the desire this gives you. I can feel the fine line between your pleasure and pain," he whispered in her ear, pinching harder until she moaned.

"Now your turn," he said, lying on his back.

Leaning over him, she kissed his lips and allowed her hand to slowly move down his chest, stopping at his waist. She backed away, but not before Sarik seized her hand and moved it to his groin.

"Reach out, Jael, feel my pleasure." He groaned. Letting go of her hand, he left her to explore on her own.

The excitement built in Sarik with each passing graze of her fingers. The more she reached within him, the more his pleasure became hers. She understood her purpose. Without restraint, she followed every pent-up desire within her and Sarik until both were consumed with unbridled bliss. Their passions fulfilled, they lay sated in each other's arms until sleep over took them.

~~~

The henge was finally in sight. Dugun and his men had three days to find what they were looking for before the precession arrived. They set up a small camp then immediately went to work. Dugun carefully plotted the location on his map. He looked around from the top of the henge for disturbances in the ground, but it had been eighteen years since the box was hidden at the burial of Jael's mother Mila. After several minutes, Dugun dug his first hole, digging deeper and deeper until he came to the conclusion he must be in the wrong spot. He dug another hole and then another and another until he gave up for the night. Frustrated he didn't find what he was looking for, he ordered his men to stay up all night and dig until they found the box.

By morning, his men lay exhausted at the top of the henge. Holes littered the land, but still they found nothing. Convinced his men were being lazy, Dugun rushed up the mound to reprimand them. He climbed to the top and stormed towards the men. Halfway there he tripped on one of the holes and landed face first in the dirt. His men laughed, but their gaiety was short lived. When he got up, he pulled his sword in a fit of rage, and they took arms against him. Before the first sword could be swung, a voice boomed across the mound.

"Dugun, have you lost your mind?" the man yelled, getting Dugun's attention.

It was the captain of his father's army standing at the base of the henge. Forgetting his anger, Dugun sheathed his sword and walked down to the bottom. The other men followed him and sat around the small fire that burned between the tents.

The captain pulled Dugun aside and spoke in a low voice, "I have bad news. Your father is dead, Dugun. You need to come home."

Dugun replied, "I'll go home when I've found what I came here for and no sooner."

Taken back by Dugun's reaction, the captain watched him walk away. "You're the clan laird now, Dugun, and your place is with your people during their time of need," he shouted.

Turning around on his heels, Dugun stalked back towards the man and grabbed him by the front of his tunic. "Don't tell me where my place is, old man!" he yelled through gritted teeth before dropping the captain back on his feet.

As the captain rode away, the other men decided he was right. They left all their belongings and abandoned the camp before Dugun knew what happened.

"I'll have you all executed!" Dugun screamed at the top of his lungs into the forest before grabbing the shovel and making his way to the top of the henge.

Dugun excavated the hill until his hands blistered and bled. He pulled the map out again, and in the moonlight he looked for a reason why the box was not where the map was marked. Frustrated he lifted it above his head and began to tear it in half. But, as moonlight hit the back of the map, symbols appeared where there had been none. The key to the map and the location of the box were shown through the moon marks. Dugun laughed and lifted the shovel once more.

He picked up a small silver box not much wider than his hand. It was covered in carvings with strange symbols on the cover, but there was no visible lock and the lid would not open. Dugun placed the box in his bag and headed home, leaving everything behind.

～

The sun crested over the hills casting a pale pink light across the front of Jael and Sarik's tent. The henge was still half day's ride away. Jael woke up naked and tangled in Sarik's limbs just as she had the last three nights; only this time she woke before him. As he slept, she brushed her hand a crossed his defined chest, feeling every ripple on its way down until she reached an area that caused him to stir and clasp her hand before it went any lower.

"Have mercy, woman," he sleepily moaned.

"Did I not show you enough mercy last night when I satisfied all of your, "God pleases"?" she teased.

He chuckled and rolled her over so his muscular body loomed over her, pinning her arms above her with one hand. She countered his move by wrapping her legs around his waist before he could pin them too.

"I like this new game of Kiss and Beg you taught me— especially when you're the one begging," she taunted as she squeezed her legs tighter around him.

He let go of her arms and rolled onto his back. He let out a deep breath. "As much as I would love to play games with you this morning, we have business to take care of." He kissed her on the cheek then got out of bed.

Jael sighed watching his naked perfection dig through his bag for clean clothes. She lay on her side, head in her hand, and thought of their lovemaking.

"Cut it out, Jael." He laughed as he dressed. "Did you forget I can hear your thoughts?"

Smiling, she raised her brow. "No, I remember that fact quite well."

"Well, you need to get dressed, and by the way, I do have a nice ass," Sarik added, tossing her clothes to her.

Just as they climbed out of the tent, one of the crewmen from the shuttle walked towards them from the woods. It must have been important because he was still dressed in his crew jumper and not native clothing.

"Your Highness," he said, slightly winded as he bowed. "There has been recent activity at the henge. We found tents and gear near the front and the top is littered with holes. The place looks like a mess, so we left a crew there to clean it up before you arrive," he explained.

"Thank you. I would hate for the clan to arrive to such desecration. I want the shuttle captain to do a wide sweep of the area and see if he can't track the culprit," Sarik commanded then put his arm around Jael.

"If you help me break down your tent, I can get it out of here now and not have to wait for help," he said.

By the time they got the tent and gear packed up, Salima arrived to tell them the clan was ready to move. Jael told

Salima about the digging at the henge. Worry washed over her face.

"I know what they're looking for. If they found it, we're in big trouble—especially you." Salima pointed to Jael.

"Tell me everything you know," Jael demanded.

"You mom had a recording stone mounted in a necklace. She recorded details of your conception, so the information could be passed to you should anything happen to her and Rowe. It was information meant for you only. That necklace is proof Rowe is not your father," Salima explained, trying to keep her voice low.

"Whoever took the necklace knew exactly what they were looking for and knows how to view the stone. There's one of our kind working against us, Salima, and we need to find them before Atlantis and Jael are exposed."

"It's nothing that can't wait until after your father has been laid to rest," replied Sarik.

"Judging by your worried mind, Sarik, I believe I have much to be concerned with. But I have to trust the clan will not be so quick to condemn me or my husband, whom they should be thankful to," stated Jael.

"As much as I trust your clan, I'm not foolish enough to believe that if they found out about your real father, they would still see things as they do now. We'll no longer be Laird and Lady of Eir if it's not our birthright," Sarik explained.

"They'll always love me and the fact I'm not Rowe's natural born child makes him no less my father," she declared.

"I have no doubt Rowe loved you. Otherwise, he would not have offered your hand to me. But, there are many in your clan who don't know you and those are the ones who'll turn on you if they think you're a witch or demon."

"I hate to butt in on your debate, but the clan is waiting on you two. And we need to get to the henge before noon. I feel a storm on the horizon." Salima looked up at the clouds overhead.

~~

They reached the henge as it began to snow. The men set up the camp while the women cooked the solstice feast. Sarik and Jael were joined by Tam, Lenni, Edric, and Halis in the main tent.

"Does anyone know why Betta and Haro are not here?" asked Sarik, sitting on one of the logs placed by the long fire in the middle of the big tent.

"None of us were there when they left. I'll ask my dad to see if he knows," said Tam, getting up from the log.

"I wish Wren and Betta were here." Lenni sighed, leaning her head on Jael's shoulder as she held her hand for comfort.

"Me too," replied Jael softly.

When Tam returned he walked straight to Sarik and whispered something in his ear. Sarik jumped up and walked out of the tent with Tam close on his heels. Kale and Jaren were in front of the henge lighting the torches that framed the entrance of the burial mound. The snow fell heavily and the wind howled as it blew across the front of the quartz wall. Sarik waited for them to light the last torch before inquiring about Haro.

"Did Haro give a reason for leaving?" Sarik asked.

The torch in Kale's hand cast an eerie shadow across his face. "No. As soon as he heard you were coming, he and Betta left. I don't even know where they went," he said.

"How long have you known him?"

"I met him at Betta's wedding and have only talked to him on a handful of occasions. To be blunt, the boy is a complete idiot. I never heard him say a single thing to make me think otherwise."

"But why would he run from me?" Sarik pondered.

"You're not the only one who finds it odd they aren't here. There's much talk among the clan members about his strange behavior. Come to think of it, no one in the clan knew him before the wedding. All we knew was that he lived in Hem and was supposedly from a prominent family, but no one had heard of them and none of his relations came to the wedding," stated Jaren.

The cogs in Sarik's mind turned. There had to be a connection between the missing box at the henge and Haro's sudden departure.

Chapter 13

After the ceremony, Sarik followed the priestesses back to the shuttle. He walked on board and sat in the chair next to the captain in the cockpit.

"Did you track the looter?" asked Sarik.

The captain pulled up a map of the entire island on a large holo screen and showed Sarik the trail the culprit made while they followed him from afar. It led from the henge into Canulis. Once well over the border, the thief stopped for the night and hadn't moved since. They would resume surveillance after they dropped the priestesses back on Hy-Brasil.

"Captain Ross will be my replacement tomorrow. He requested to help with the precession back to Halor. In the meantime, they're tracking your thief from space, so we won't lose him," reported the captain. "I almost forgot, the Laird of Canulis is dead. We don't have any information on how, but I suspect it was at the hands of the same person who killed the laird's oldest son," he added.

Sarik grimaced as he passed his hand over his face. Dugun would be in charge of the old laird's army and still believed he was the rightful heir of Eir. Any thought of a peaceful resolution was dashed.

"Please keep me informed if you find out any more information. I'll need as much leverage as I can get if I'm going to convince the clan of Canulis not to follow their new laird," directed Sarik, leaning onto the center console with his elbow and rubbing his forehead with his fingers to lessen the stress in his furrowed brow.

"Understood," the captain replied. "I'll pass down the information to Captain Ross. We have a couple of crew members who have gone native and wouldn't mind doing intel for us."

"Good, tell Captain Ross I'll see him in the morning. I expect to be briefed at dawn."

"Will do, your highness. Is there anything else you would like for me to relay to Captain Ross?"

"Ask him to bring a bottle or two of Cerulean Ale. I could use a drink." He sighed, sitting up then sinking into the back of the chair. After a few minutes he left the captain and his crew to attend to business and hiked back to camp.

Tam was still awake when he got back. He sat by the fire as if lost in thought when Sarik joined him. "I don't know how much your father has told you about Hy-Brasil, but it's time you were told our secret."

Tam looked at Sarik and replied, "I don't understand."

"Tomorrow morn you'll accompany me and all will be explained. Until then, we could both use some sleep."

"I tried to sleep, but every time I get near Lenni, I'm assaulted by her emotions as if they're my own. It's leaving me drained," Tam croaked.

"Jael knows a way to block that. I'm sure she'd be more than happy to help you. Otherwise, if Lenni should become pregnant, you'll find yourself weeping at every rainbow and butterfly." Sarik laughed.

"God forbid. I'm already on the verge of weeping and laughing as it is."

"Lenni's emotions are affecting everyone."

"Don't tell anyone, but sometimes she can see things that are to come. She saved my life on the way to Blackrock. She knew we were going to be attacked before it happened."

"Very interesting. Has she had any other visions?"

"None that she has told me of."

"Well keep me informed if she does. Even if it seems to be irrelevant, I'd like to know about it. Her gift could help protect the clan."

"I'm worried about her gift. I almost lost her to a mystery man she insisted was her husband to be. That was until she realized he was already married to Jael." Tam laughed as he gazed into the fire and poked at it with a stick.

Tam's admission shocked Sarik. He could've been the reason Lenni dreamed about him. He reached out many times, without success, to contact Jael before he agreed to the betrothal and even earlier when he attempted to find out what was so special about Rowe's daughter that it kept Salima from him. It was possible he reached Lenni instead and made her believe he was meant for her. He would tell Tam tomorrow after they both had a good night's sleep and more privacy. "Well, I'm glad she came to her senses. It's obvious she belongs with you." He stretched his legs in front of him then stood.

Throwing the stick into the fire, Tam joined Lenni in the smaller, less crowed tent they shared with Halis and Edric. Glad that Lenni was asleep, he crawled next to her under the covers and easily drifted off now that his mind was at peace from her emotional assault.

Sarik had no such luck. Jael waited for him in their private tent. It wasn't the one they slept in while traveling, but a cozy native tent.

"You look like hell." She sat up, noticing the dark circles under his eyes.

"I was about to tell you the same thing." He chuckled halfheartedly.

"Lenni is wearing me out," she said, throwing herself back down on the mattress with an audible sigh.

"Tam said the same thing. I believe she's a telepath and is unconsciously projecting her feelings. I told Tam you'd help him learn to block her out, until someone can teach her to control it," he said, removing his clothes and climbing next to her in the bed. "You're freezing!" A shiver ran through him as her cold flesh met his.

"I'm too tired to make heat. I was hoping you could warm me." She snuggled closer to his warm body.

He concentrated on the air around them and within seconds they were both warm, and fast asleep.

~~~

The sun was still below the hills when Sarik and Tam left the camp and headed to the shuttle. On their walk there Sarik explained to Tam that Atlantis was really a starship, and its people were not of this earth. Tam listened in disbelief while Sarik continued, "My people have the ability to manipulate energy." He opened his hand in front of him, palm up. Water droplets from the morning mist pooled in his hand then overflowed like a waterfall.

"How did you do that?"

Sarik threw the handful of water up and suspended it in the air before them. A couple seconds later he let it fall to the ground. "I'm moving the energy around the water."

By the time they reached the shuttle Tam's mind was spinning. They walked onboard and sat at a small table in a private room along with Captain Ross.

"Your looter is on the move. Should we pick him up?" asked Captain Ross

"No. I need to know who's behind all of this. Just have your men keep tabs on him." Sarik pulled up the image in front of them and watched as the lone rider made his way through the forest. Tam stood behind him with his eyes wide open as he attempted to wrap his head around what he was seeing.

"I have four men in Canulis; two in the capital at Kilcur and two moles in the army at Annoc. We got word back from Kilcur this morning that the new laird is nowhere to be found. The old laird's captain of the guards returned from somewhere north complaining about Dugun's lack of propriety when he told him of his father's death," Captain Ross relayed.

"Do we know where Dugun is?" asked Tam.

"No, but we're actively looking for him. We'll let you know when he's located."

"For now, just fly ahead of us and make sure the forest is clear. Tam, I want you to ride with Captain Ross and use this time to ask him whatever questions you may have about Hy-Brasil. As my council, I'll expect you to be able to see things from all angles—including the ones of my people and Jael's." Sarik knew this was a lot for Tam to grasp, but mentally justified the method. Immersion was the best way to for Tam to learn.

"You want me to fly in this big metal monstrosity?" said Tam, his voice laced with a mixture of nervousness and excitement.

"Yes and get used to it. It's the way Jael and I will travel whenever possible."

"Jael knows about all of this?"

Sarik put his hand on the back of his neck and looked at the ground for a second before he made eye contact with Tam and snorted. "How do I explain Jael? Let's just say, Rowe had his reasons for betrothing Jael to me and my protection was only one of them."

"So she's like you?"

"More precisely, she's like Salima, who's a Jinn. They coexist with us in Hy-Brasil."

"How will you explain my absences to Lenni?"

"I'll tell her I sent you ahead to scout, and you can meet up with us when we stop for the evening," said Sarik, getting up from the table.

"There's nothing to worry about, Tam. I haven't crashed in years," joked Captain Ross.

"You're kidding, right?" Tam stammered, getting up from his chair and following Captain Ross to the cockpit. He glanced back before Sarik disembarked. Tam's expression had "help me" written all over it. Sarik gave him a reassuring smile as he walked away.

Captain Ross sat in his chair and gave Tam a sideways grin as he started the engines. Tam looked back at the door and watched it close. He white knuckled the back of the copilot's seat as he stood behind it.

"I'm joking," laughed the captain.

By the time he got back to camp, the clan was ready to move. The snow from the night before began to melt from the sun now hanging right over the tops of the hills. Sarik quickly consulted Jael, Kale, and Jaren about the day's journey. Sarik, Jael, Salima and Var would take the lead and Kale, Jaren and Tal would bring up the rear.

By noon the snow completely melted, leaving a muddy mess on the trail, but the clan was grateful for the warm sunny day. They made better time than they did on the way over so Salima and Sarik looked for a new area to camp. Sarik got in touch with Captain Ross telepathically and asked for coordinates to the nearest clearing. He and Salima rode to the location to make sure it would be suitable for their needs.

When they got there, the shuttle was waiting for them. The door opened and Tam walked out to greet Sarik.

"How was the flight?" Sarik asked.

"Scary, but incredible! There's so much to learn. I don't know where to begin." He spoke like a kid on his first pony ride, eyes flashing and hands gesturing unable to contain his excitement.

"I'm glad it agrees with you. Jaren lost his lunch on his first ride." Sarik laughed.

"Jaren has flown?"

"Yes, so has your father—many times."

"I'm surprised he's been able to keep everything a secret for so long."

"Are you going to wait here or go back out with Captain Ross?" asked Sarik.

"I'm going back out with the shuttle. I'll have them drop me off right before the clan gets here. There are so many things I want to ask Captain Ross." Tam waved before he disappeared inside the shuttle.

Sarik spent the rest of the afternoon guiding the clan to the clearing. Jael loaned her horse to an elderly couple who had a difficult time keeping up. She talked to the clan as she walked amongst them and addressed their concerns.

~~~

It was almost morning when Dugun arrived at the camp in Annoc. Without hesitation, he grabbed the box from his bag and brought it to the main tent. "Here's your box," he grumbled, throwing it onto the table. "I don't know how you plan on opening it. There's no lock."

The man ran his hand across the top of the box, flames dancing across his fingertips. The box made an audible click. The flames disappeared from his hands and he smiled as he raised the lid. Inside he saw the center stone of the necklace glowing blue and grimaced as he pulled it out of the box. He held it behind the candle on his desk and inspected every inch of it in the light. The faceted gem was an odd shaped blue and green memory stone. It was wrapped in silver with tiny silver beads and seed pearls laced throughout. A small carved mermaid curled across one of the upper corners—a sign it had been made in Atlantis. Bringing the piece to his nose, he inhaled the scent of the black leather cord that it hung from before returning it to the box and shutting the lid.

"Now get yourself to Kilcur. The clan is wondering where their new laird is. I'll summon you when you're needed," he said, dismissing Dugun.

Exhausted, Dugun climbed onto a new horse and began the trip to his family home in Kilcur. When he arrived, Wren waited for him with open arms. He ignored her and went straight to bed.

He tossed and turned all night and well into the morning as dreams of death and destructions over took his slumber. He bolted up in his bed, heart racing out of his chest at his latest nightmare—fire. His master perched on the cliffs at Annoc in his blue demon-like form, laughing while the world burned around him. Heartless and without discrimination, he destroyed both the men of Eir and Canulis alike.

Dugun got out of bed, nausea overtaking him. He wiped the cold sweat from his brow and wandered to the window, inhaling the cold air that seeped in around shutters. His ambitions blinded him. As if being struck by lightning, clarity penetrated his mind and the guilt from the deaths he caused overwhelmed him. Dugun leaned against the stone wall, attempting to steady himself, but as everything came crashing in, he slid down the wall and sobbed—his arms wrapped around his knees like a child. His beloved father and brother were dead because of him, and although it was not at his own hands, he was responsible.

Mortified, he crawled across the floor and retrieved his sword from the table where it sat, the very one he attempted to kill Tam with. He plunged the blade into his heart and felt the guilt and blood seep away into blackness.

~~~

Half way through the day, Sarik got word of Dugun's suicide. Concerned about Wren, a party consisting of Jael, Lenni, himself, Salima, Tal and a hand full of guards, broke off from the group and made their way to Kilcur. It was nightfall by the time they made it to the gates of Kilcur, and to Sarik's surprise, they went unchallenged the whole trip across Canulis. As soon as they dismounted, Wren rushed out of the front door and confronted them.

Hands fisted, she screamed, "How dare you show up here? This is entirely your fault. I'm the oldest, and it was Dugun's place to be Laird of Eir, not you!" She accused, beating her fists into Sarik's chest.

Instead of responding with anger, Sarik reached his arms around and embraced her like a father comforting a child. Petting her hair gently, he said, "Wren, I'm truly sorry for your loss. Your family is here for you."

The stiffness in her body relaxed as she began sobbed. Sarik released his embrace only to be replaced with Lenni and Jael who walked her into the house. Sarik grabbed his saddlebag from the horse when the old laird's guard captain addressed him.

"Are you prince Sarik of Hy-Brasil?" he asked.

"Yes," Sarik responded apprehensively to the man's question.

The captain bowed. "I'm Leif, captain of the army. I fear for the people of Canulis, your highness. Ever since Dugun began to associate with Haro, we've had one accident after another. And now we're left without a laird. Our army has been taken over by Haro, and the remaining clansmen are in chaos—not knowing which side to take. They debate about whether they should follow Haro to war, despite their lack of grievances, or join Eir and fight against their own. Most would choose to do neither, but Haro will kill them."

Sarik was shocked, but now he had the name of their traitor—Betta's husband, Haro. "If I lead, will your men follow?" he asked.

"They would if you could guarantee peace with Eir without subjugation," Leif replied.

"Then I accept, but only if you continue to lead them, Leif. Tonight I'd like to meet with all the town and guard leaders you can muster. I'm all for a peaceful resolution, if there is one to be had," said Sarik.

"Thank you, your highness," he said, giving a quick bow and leaving.

Sarik walked into the house, which was somewhat crowded with clans people there for the laird's burial. Wren, Lenni and Jael sat in a private room that had been used by the old laird for more intimate meetings. Sarik put his bag down in an empty bedroom and joined the girls, who were still trying to calm Wren.

"Wren, as Lady of Canulis it's your job to speak with your people. Right now they're looking for reassurance that all is not lost." Jael clasped her sister's hand.

"What am I supposed to tell them?" she sobbed.

"Tell them the truth. Remind them that you have not forgotten them and that Eir is an ally and not an enemy," Jael replied.

Wren wiped the tears from her face and took in a deep breath. "I'm not strong enough to lead these people. Haro has made a complete mess of everything. He promised Dugun the Lairdship of Canulis and Eir if Dugun helped him take over the northern clans," she confessed. "I don't believe Dugun knew it would be at the expense of his brother and father, not to mention our father." She hung her head down in shame knowing she could've prevented much of this if her own ambition to be Lady of Eir had not gotten in the way.

"What's done is done, and if you have any inclination to ease your conscience, then you'll help to make things right between Canulis and Eir." Sarik wouldn't allow Wren to become weak and back out of her responsibilities. "Get yourself cleaned up. You'll address your guests in the great hall within the hour." Sarik stood and left the room.

He checked on Salima and Tal who were making camp with the rest of his men, outside the great house's walls. "Tal, I need you to listen for anyone who might be a supporter of Haro. If you need to take mist form, do so in the nearby woods and take Fairen with you for protection. Jael and I are meeting with the prominent clansmen tonight, and I want to make sure we don't have spies or assassins among them."

"Haro is our traitor?" she asked.

"Yes, and I have reason to believe he's the one with the recording stone. Apparently, this is all part of a bigger plan to take over all of the northern clans. He's been using Dugun as a puppet this whole time."

"I've had my suspicions about him. Although, I find it odd that Betta has been quiet about all of this. If he's one of our kind, why would he go through such lengths to acquire land? None of it makes sense," said Salima.

"I don't understand either. Most of our laws for Earth were written to prevent hostile takeovers. I know he's not from Hy-Brasil, because I checked for Nauss and Jinn who have gone native before we got here and didn't notice anything unusual. I'll ask Captain Ross to check again, maybe I missed something."

"You were supposed to talk with Lenni back in Halor. She might have some useful information. It's safe to say that whoever Haro is, he's very good at covering his tracks," Salima suggested.

"I'll do that now. In the meantime, I give you and Tal permission to infiltrate the minds of anyone you find suspicious," he said as he walked away.

Tal removed any unnecessary clothing she had on. "You can give all the permission you like, but that doesn't mean I'm willing to," she said under her breath, watching him go.

When he was halfway to the house, he glanced back at Tal. He shook his head and chuckled at her. He saw her and Fairen holding hands as they entered the woods. "How could I've missed their romance going on right under my nose?" he mused.

Wren was ready to address the throng of people in the congested great hall. Despite her nervousness, she thanked everyone for their concern and sympathy then reassured them she would not abandon them. After her speech everyone departed except those who were meeting with Sarik and Jael at Leif's request.

"I'd like to say thank you for coming," he started. "I know it's late in the hour, but there's much to be discussed and little time to discuss it. As you all know, there's been a rash of recent events that have torn these lands in two. It's my deepest regret that you have lost not one laird but two—and all for the greed of one man. I want you to know that you have an ally in Eir. It's in both our interests to cooperate and rid

ourselves of the disease that plagues our lands. Leif has
volunteered to command Canulis, and Lady Jael and I will be
working with him to find a peaceful resolution. All I ask is
that you trust us to do what is right by your clan and support
our effort."

They spent the whole night negotiating the terms of this
alliance. The more time they spent with Sarik and Jael, the
more they trusted them. In the end, they all agreed to support
the cause.

Chapter 14

Dawn peeked through the forest by the time the meeting concluded. Sarik stepped outside and inhaled the cold winter air. He made his way to his men's camp and sat on one of the logs near the fire to warm his hands. One of his men brought him a hot cup of warm broth to drink while he waited to hear the report from last night.

Fairen looked rough with dark circles beneath his glossed over eyes, reminding Sarik that he was only human. "Any news from last night?" asked Sarik.

Tal stretched her long legs out in front of her. "There were a couple of Haro's supporters, but none were part of your meeting. I have the shuttle tracking them to see if see if any report back to Haro. Should I stop them?" she asked.

"No, it won't be necessary, I'm sure Haro already knows I'm here. I need to talk to Captain Ross and find out if he's heard anything from our people in Annoc," he said.

"Sarik, you have no idea how scared these people are. Some have even talked of fleeing to the south with the barbarians. They are desperate, and desperate people do stupid things. It's not enough to have Wren and Captain Leif leading them; they want a leader who can hold this clan together. I suggest you take the post before somebody else does," informed Salima.

Sarik sighed and ran his fingers through his hair. "This isn't what I signed up for, Salima, but I'll take it under consideration."

~~~

Jael woke to the sound of Wren crying in her sleep. She dressed and went to the great hall. When she got to the doorway, she noticed Sarik sitting alone at one of the tables. It was obvious from his slacked posture and furrowed brow that he was brooding over the talks from the previous night. She walked up behind him and massaged his strong shoulders.

"I missed you," she whispered in his ear.

"I missed you too," he said as he reached across his shoulder to clasp her hand.

She walked around and sat next to him on the bench. He put his arm around her shoulder and pulled her closer. "Sarik, Wren's falling apart. I worry she may take her own life." She sighed.

"There's nothing I can do for her, Jael. She has made her bed and now she must lie in it, such is life," he responded coldly.

She pulled away and looked at him, taken aback by his response. "She's my sister!"

"I'm sorry, but it's hard to have sympathy for a person who willingly allowed the death of others to elevate her own position. Not that I wish her ill, but don't expect me to feel sorry for her," he snapped.

She took a deep breath and put her forehead on the table. "This whole situation is messed up."

Placing his hand on her back, he rubbed her shoulders. "I'm sorry. I'm tired and there's a lot I still need to do. I didn't mean to upset you," he said with a certain sadness then kissed the top of her head.

"I wish this was all over, and we could go back to Atlantis. I could use a hot bath and a glass of Cerulean ale." She sighed, but sat back up straight.

"The stress is getting to both of us. But part of being a leader is sacrifice, so for now, we'll have to settle on a warm wash and a cup of mead and be thankful we have a roof over our heads while the clan is still making its way home."

"You have a point, Sarik." She clasped his hand and kissed his cheek.

By noon, Leif returned to the great house. He, Sarik, and Fairen spent much of the day planning a defensive move to keep the army at Annoc from moving any further into Canulis. They'd move troops to the west as early as that evening. The only problem was that Eir would be left wide open, its people were still three days away from Annoc and tired from the trip to the henge and back. At this point, the only action Sarik could take was to commandeer another shuttle and have it keep watch over the border as a precaution.

When they were finished, Sarik called for Jael to meet him at the stable. She spent the entire day talking with the locals, a job that was meant for the Lady of Canulis, but Jael filled in when Wren failed to do so. He had a horse ready for her when she arrived. They rode into the woods, and Jael followed him without question. After twenty minutes they reached the shuttle where Captain Ross waited for them.

Once aboard, they sat down at a small table with fancy fabric covering it and candles flickering in the darkened shuttle. Music played in the background while Captain Ross poured them each a glass of Cerulean Ale then left the room. Jael inhaled its flowery aroma before taking her first sip and sinking back in her chair.

Reaching across the table, Sarik took her hand. He gently rubbed his thumb across hers and smiled. "For the next two hours you have my whole, undivided attention."

"Sarik, when all this is over can we go home? Back to Atlantis?"

Jael tugged on his heart strings when she called Atlantis home, but the unfortunate reality of the situation was that Eir and now Canulis would have to become their home. It was the first time in Sarik's life he had to give up something so precious to be responsible, a painful lesson his father had been trying to teach him his whole life.

"Jael, I don't know when we'll be able to return. But I promise one day we will." He squeezed her hand and grinned. "Now enough with the depressing stuff, we're here to have fun."

Downing the rest of her drink, she stood, walked over to Sarik, and sat on his lap with her arms around his neck and head resting on his shoulder. Without warning the shuttle fired up and took off. Startled, Jael squeezed her arms tighter as he put his arms around her waist.

Baffled by the shuttles unplanned take off, Sarik mumbled, "I wonder what this is all about?"

As the shuttle climbed higher and higher, curiosity got the best of him. Moving Jael off his lap, he took her hand and led her to the cockpit where Captain Ross and another crewmember sat flying the shuttle.

"What's going on?" questioned Sarik.

"We spotted locals in the woods closing in on us, so we had to leave," replied Captain Ross, continuing to climb above the clouds.

"Is there any reason we're climbing?" Sarik asked.

"I figured since we had to waste some time, we could take a little trip north. The aurora is unusually active tonight. I thought the Lady Jael would enjoy her first trip into space," he responded.

Squeezing Sarik's hand in excitement, Jael squealed. "We're going into space?"

"It appears so," he replied, sitting in the third seat and pulled her back on his lap.

With her eyes wide open, Jael looked outside the cockpit window. Within minutes she could feel her bottom rise up off of Sarik's lap. He tightened his grip around her waist and pulled her back against him before Captain Ross turned on the artificial gravity. Soon the shuttle stopped moving and the atmosphere below danced with colors as charged partials illuminated the night sky.

"It's the most beautiful thing I've ever seen," she squealed, standing up and leaning closer to the window.

"Yes, you are," said Sarik, drinking in Jael's happiness.

Jael looked at him and laughed. "Is this what it's like to travel in space?"

"Sometimes yes, but not all of the time. When the big ship has to travel long distances, the stars become a big blur until it stops," he said.

"This is so amazing. I wish we could stay here forever." She sighed.

Sarik walked to the back and retrieved their glasses and the bottle of liquor. When he returned to the cockpit, the captain could tell by the lusty look in his eyes that his presence was no longer required. So he and the co-pilot left, shutting the door behind them.

Sarik handed Jael her drink, her eyes still glued to the outside view. She didn't notice Sarik unlacing her dress while she sipped her drink. He admired Jael's naked form through her shift, her dress puddled on the floor around her ankles. Moving her hair aside, he kissed the back of her neck, and his hand reached around to firmly clutch her breast.

Jael let out a small moan then turned to face Sarik. Her head was dizzy with drink and fervor. She removed his tunic and leather pants while he hastened to remove her shift. Pushing him back into the center chair and throwing up the arm rests, Jael straddled Sarik's lap, her inhibitions gone. The only thought on her mind was Sarik's pleasure. She wrapped her arms around his neck and kissed him on the lips, her tongue engaging with his until the burning between her thighs begged for attention. She moved up and down against his hardness, absorbing his excitement into her.

Moaning, Sarik could feel Jael's wetness against his shaft as she moved against him. He fingered her breast then leaned down to take her nipple between his teeth. Jael moved up higher and grabbed his hair pulling him closer before lowering herself slowly, finally allowing him entry. She moved so her sensitive spot rubbed against his groin with every stroke, but when Sarik grabbed her by the hips to take control, she moved his hands away and pushed him harder against the back of the chair.

"I see we're playing the whore tonight," he growled.

She stopped moving, pulled away, and slapped his face.

He laughed, rubbing the spot where she hit him. "So you want to play rough, do you?"

Without a word, she gave him a let-me-see-you-try glare. Next thing she knew, Sarik stood and pinned her against the center console with one of her legs over his shoulder.

The harder and faster he moved the more excited she became, looping her free leg around the small of his back to pull him closer. Buttons and switches dug into her as Sarik's full weight pushed down on her with each stroke, until finally she couldn't hold back any more.

"Oh...God...YES!" she yelled.

Sarik roared giving one last hard push, tumbling them both over the edge.

~~

The shuttle dropped them off in the field where they left the horses, but Jael drank so much she could no longer feel her face. Sarik let her ride in front of him on his horse and tethered her horse to his. She laughed most of the way back until she passed out in his arms.

Tal, Salima, and Fairen waited for them when they got back. After laying Jael down in Tal's tent, Sarik joined them by the fire.

"I got intel from Captain Ross. It appears Haro is a Jinn, but nobody knew of him. I know you've met him, Salima. I'm surprised you didn't know he was Jinn."

"As am I, Sarik. Whoever he is, he can keep the others from sensing him, which is not an easy task."

"How do we get rid of him?" Fairen sounded in.

Salima answered, "According to our laws, he can be forcibly removed, but since we're refugees in Hy-Brasil, we have to follow their rules. And if I'm not mistaken, that would mean waiting until he has started a war. Unless we can prove he is responsible for the deaths of Rowe and the others."

"That might be a bit difficult now that the person who could testify against him has killed himself," said Fairen.

"That does put a damper on things. I'll see if my father will allow us to make a move against Haro on the grounds of intent. Otherwise, I believe we're on our own," stated Sarik.

"I know of a couple of other Jinn who would be willing to help us if we need them," added Tal.

Standing, Sarik stretched his arms above his head and yawned. " I need some sleep," he said, then crawled into Tal's tent with Jael.

Tal looked at Fairen and made a face. "I believe I just lost my tent. Now where am I supposed to sleep?"

He gave an evil side grin before answering, "Last one to the tent has to tend the horses." As he got up to run, Tal turned into a swift wisp of smoke. "No fair," he yelled, as she smiled at him from the tent entrance.

~~

"Wake up," yelled Lenni as she pounded her hand on the top of the tent, half panicked.

Sarik opened the flap and bellowed, "Enough already, we're up."

Lenni blushed when she noticed Sarik wasn't clothed, so she turned away and spoke, "Wren is missing!"

Shaking her head, Jael handed Sarik his pants and shirt. "What do you mean missing?"

"She's nowhere to be found, and her pony is missing too."

"Did anyone see her leave?" Sarik asked, tying the last lace on his tunic.

"Only the boy who tends the horses, but he didn't think to ask where she was going."

Groaning, Sarik put his boots on and walked away beckoning Salima to follow him. "I need to reach Captain Ross, but he's out of my range," he said, pacing the nearby woods with balled fists.

"Do you know which direction he went?" she questioned, watching him walk back and forth in front of her.

"He's following the clan home, so he should be west of here."

"I should be able to relay with Tal. What do you want her to tell him?"

"I need him to scan the area between here and Annoc. Look for a lone rider on a stag pony," he growled. "I swear, Rowe, your daughters will be the death of me," he said under his breath.

After a couple of minutes the message was relayed, and the shuttle made its way back to Canulis to look for Wren. Sarik and Salima returned to the camp where Jael tried to calm Lenni.

"How can you be so callous!" Lenni yelled, tears streaming down her face.

"She's a grown woman who left of her own accord. How am I supposed to worry for her when in my heart I know she's off to join the enemy?" Jael reasoned calmly from her seat by the fire.

"She's not in her right mind." Lenni walked to where Jael sat and joined her on the log.

"She has mind enough to ride a pony to Annoc alone, Lenni," retorted Jael. "Dugun has not yet been buried, and still she runs to Haro. And where is Betta? She's the one we should all be concerned about."

Lenni paused taking in what Jael was alluding to. "I never thought about that, and now I have two sisters to worry about. I believed her to be safe in Hem, but now that you mention it, things have been very odd with her the last couple of years. Even when I went to visit, she seemed like a complete stranger." Lenni stared at the fire in deep thought.

"I never did understand how she could stay away so long and miss father's burial. That's not in Betta's nature," Jael said as Sarik and Salima joined them.

"I hate to end your discussion, but now that Wren is gone, there's no one in charge of the clan. Jael, I need your help hashing out a plan before this goes to crisis. We need to work something out with Leif, because I'm already feeling overwhelmed leading Eir," he groaned.

Jael clasped his hand and squeezed. "It'll be okay. I think I have the solution to our problem. I noticed Hy-Brasil was divided into districts that had their own leaders and your father ruled over them. Couldn't we do something similar? You could be King, like your father, and Tam could rule Eir in your place and Leif would be a worthy choice for Canulis. He already has the respect of his people."

"I knew there was a reason your father wanted you to rule. You're a genius." Sarik kissed the top of her head.

As if on cue, Leif entered their camp. "I couldn't find you at the laird's house," he said.

"I was just about to look for you," said Sarik, as he stood and walked towards the house holding Jael's hand with Leif on their heels. "Has your clan considered a replacement?"

"There has been much discussion about the matter, and we keep coming to the same conclusion," Leif said.

"And what is that?"

"With our army split to the west and the constant problems to the south with the barbarians, we've concluded we need Eir's protection to survive," he revealed nervously.

Sarik took a deep breath and let it out as he tried to relax the tension building in his neck. "Get to your point, man."

"The clan elders wish for Canulis to be annexed by Eir," he blurted out.

"That's not something I would consider until we've debated and drawn contracts. Not that I'm unwilling to add Canulis to my kingdom, it just needs to be done legally and with the majority of the clans consent. I refuse to have internal battles with members who do not wish me to lead them," he said bluntly as they entered the great hall.

"I understand. That's why the elders have called a clan meeting here tonight."

"Very well, Leif. But, understand this," he paused to look him in the eyes, "you might find yourself in a position you did not desire. I will expect you to give me nothing less than your best."

"For my clan I'd give my life and suffer whatever job you demand of me," he proclaimed.

"That's a good man. Now for the more pressing matters, where's breakfast?" jested Sarik, sitting down at one of the long tables in the great hall. To his surprise the house was still running as if it had a master within its walls. It was a good sign that the old laird of Canulis ran a tight ship and his staff delivered nothing less even without supervision.

Jael and Lenni joined them at the table. Lenni moped about missing Tam. Much to her glee, Tam arrived in the great hall just as they were cleaning up breakfast. Lenni dropped everything in her hands and ran to greet him. She threw her arms around his neck so hard she almost knocked him over.

"What are you doing here?" she asked, smiling from ear to ear.

"My father and Jaren have things well in hand, so I came to get my wife and bring her home." He buried his face in her hair and inhaled deeply, having missed her scent more than he ever thought possible.

Lenni melted against him as his presence erased all of her previous worries.

He released his embrace and kissed her lips savoring each moment. He pulled back slightly with a smile tilting his mouth and brushed a strand of hair from her face. "I missed your beautiful face."

"Just my face?" she teased.

Tam laughed and took her by the hand. "Not just your face. I missed your constant chatter too." He pulled her over to the chairs in front of the hearth and sat down. "Now tell me everything that has happened.

Lenni babbled on cloud nine about everything that happened in the last couple days.

Before long, Sarik invaded their privacy. "I'm glad you're here, Tam." He looked at Lenni and added, "I'm sorry to take him away already, but I have pressing issues that need his assistance." He led Tam out of the great room and into the private chamber where Jael, Salima, and Fairen waited.

"Canulis has asked to be annexed by Eir. They want me to assume the duties of laird, but I think now would be a good time to make some changes that would be for the better of both clans. The first item is, rather than assimilation, I think Eir and Canulis need to keep their identities. Both lands will become part of a larger kingdom, but will maintain their ways. I'll be designating Leif as Laird of Canulis and Tam as Laird of Eir. Each will still answer to us, King Sarik and Queen Jael of Eirland. I leave open the option to subjugate the lands south of Canulis and to annex them into the kingdom."

Jael wrote as fast as she could, but Sarik spoke too fast for her to keep up. He paused just long enough for her to write his last word before beginning again. For the next couple of hours they discussed the details and decided on a plan that would be mutually beneficial for both Eir and Canulis. Jael added the last item to the treaty as the elders showed up for the meeting. Sarik laid out their plans before them, and after a few minutes of debate, the elders unanimously agreed to his solution right down to the new fortress Sarik planned to build on the cliffs just north of Annoc, the same stretch of land that was promised to him by Rowe plus the addition of a track of land in Canulis.

As the elders signed the treaty, Jael's eyes watered. She had inadvertently condemned herself and Sarik to a life away from Atlantis.

Sarik informed everyone in his party that they'd be leaving Canulis in Leif's hands and returning to Eir. Upon their arrival word came that Captain Ross had an urgent matter to discuss with him. He and Jael rode to the meadow not far from Halis and Edric's cottage.

"I'm glad you're here," the captain said. "I have information about Wren and Betta. It seems Betta is indeed missing. No one has seen her since the day before you got here. Wren has defected to Haro's side, and we have conformation that they're lovers. She may also have had a hand in some of the deaths. We're still waiting for proof from the lab that she has been exposed to water hemlock. Although it looks like she did not have a hand in Dugun's death, she's not beyond suspicion. Haro's army is well organized, but he leads by fear. If given the choice, most of his men would abandon him," he explained.

"Do you have someone in Hem looking for Betta?" Jael asked, concerned about the welfare of her sister.

"I have two men looking into it. Someone must know where she is or what might have happen to her," Captain Ross said.

"Thank you, Captain Ross," added Sarik.

"One more thing," Captain Ross said then paused as if to think. "We believe Haro is just a guise to keep us from learning the person's true identity."

"I agree," said Sarik before he and Jael got up from their seat and rode back to the house.

"Why would Wren turn against us?" she asked.

"I wish I knew. I don't believe she's one hundred percent cognizant. But that has yet to be proven," he added as doubt infiltrated his thoughts.

"The last two weeks have been a living hell, Sarik. I can't wait for things to calm down, so we can enjoy life once again." She leaned her head against his chest and took in a deep breath as she held back her tears.

"You're not the only one."   He held her until she moved away then kissed her forehead before they made their way back home.

Chapter 15

A week passed after Jael and Sarik returned to Eir. Jael spent her days in the woods with Salima and Tal learning as much as she could about her powers. Although turning into a house cat was easy, mastering the mist was quiet difficult and consumed much of her time. Tal showed her how to fight with daggers, but Jael's body was not conditioned for fighting, and she lacked the flexibility to do most of Tal's moves. She was taught how to use fire instead, a power that was useless when it came to fighting other Jinn—as they are impervious to fire—but helpful against human opponents.

Sarik and Tam worked with the army. They were thankful the weary group had a few days to recuperate from the trip to the henge before they had to move to the border near Annoc. Most of the men were farmers and hunters and required a lot of help to get them in the mentality of soldiering. The hunters had the advantage of knowing how to use a bow proficiently, but lacked the expertise to work as a group. And the farmers although capable of swinging a sword possessed little skill in doing so.

Tam joined Sarik watching a small group of bowmen attempt to shoot multiple targets. They let loose their arrows and all hit targets, but mostly the same one, leaving many targets unscathed. He let out an audible grunt, frustrated by their lack of organization.

"Tam, your clansmen are going to get slaughtered if I can't teach them how to shoot in a group," he complained.

"Well, look on the bright side, Sarik. At least the bowmen are capable of hitting their targets, even if they don't know which one to hit. If I can't get our swordsmen in shape, we won't have any left for battle—they keep wounding each other in practice." Tam laughed, trying to make light of their desperate situation.

Shaking his head, Sarik replied, "The longer we can hold off this battle the better. I don't wish to have anyone hurt, but Hy-Brasil refuses to send more support than it already has. They fear the Jinn who reside there will protest any action against their kind. I'm tired of these political games."

Tam took a deep breath to clear his mind. "I'm just glad we still have use of both shuttles and twenty or so men. The information they have gathered has been invaluable."

"At least Fairen's men are well-trained, and Leif's ability to organize his has kept us from having to deal with Canulis at all. He told me a slow trickle of men have escaped from Haro's army. They tell the most horrifying stories of what Haro does to those who leave his service." He shook his head as his eyes glassed over.

Looking to change the subject from what was sure to be a gory, graphic tale, Tam inquired, "How's Jael's training coming along?"

"Slow, painful, and tiring. I've seen little of her in the last week, and when I do, she's frustrated and exhausted. I'd have her stop, but I need to know she can defend herself if need be," Sarik replied. "And what of Lenni? Does she still wish to go north with Captain Ross' men and look for Betta?"

"Yes, but it's a sore subject. I don't want her to go. It's too dangerous even with the powers his men have. She needs to stay here and let them do their job," he complained.

"You know she'll find a way to go, and her way may not be as safe as the one proposed."

"I've taken that under consideration, but I have a hard time letting her go," Tam confessed.

"Just remember, you're dealing with one of Rowe's daughters. No isn't in their vocabulary," poked Sarik.

"Maybe I'll reconsider." Tam sighed, before being interrupted by one of the swordsmen.

"My laird, there's been an accident at the sparing field, and we need your assistance sewing up the wound," He bent over with his hands on his knees trying to catch his breath.

Tam looked back at Sarik. "You might want to show them how to fan out in an arch," he yelled as he was leaving.

"And you might want to let Lenni look for her sister before she does something stupid," Sarik shouted back.

Tam waved his hand over his head as if to ignore Sarik's suggestion and continued to make his way to the sparing field. When he got there, the scene was bloodier than he expected. The swordsman sat against a large tree with his wrist and arm wrapped in bloody cloths. As soon as Tam noticed how pale the man was, he sent someone to get Var—the wound was beyond his skills.

Var arrived and unwrapped the bandages. The cut was down to the bone and continued to bleed profusely. She concentrated on the main vein attempting to repair it as she kept her fingers pressed down tight on the pressure point higher than the wound to stop the bleeding. After several minutes the wound finally stopped bleeding, and Var worked on ridding the wound of infection before closing it up. The man lost a lot of blood, but after an hour or so the color returned to his face, and they were able to move him to his home.

Tam came to the conclusion they should avoid fighting at all cost; otherwise, he'd be sending men on a death mission. He needed his father's help, but now that he was Laird of Eir, his father felt it was his duty to train the men. So, when the time came, Kale and Jaren followed Fairen to the boarder, and left Tam.

"Alright, time to get back to practice," he yelled as the men were still milling about without direction. "And try not to hurt each other."

~~

"Jael, feel the air around you. This time remember your body is just another form of energy. Become the air. Change your energy to match that of the airs," coaxed Salima before dissolving into a wisp of smoke then reappearing behind Jael.

Jael looked with her mind at the air. Moving the energy in her own body, she attempted to mimic it. Her body faded as she intermingled with the air, becoming one with it; that was when she realized she didn't know how to move across it, so her body hung in one place like a heavy fog.

"You have to will yourself to move," said Salima, laughing at the sight of Jael's mist form hovering just over the ground. When the mist still did not move, Salima ran through it to disrupt the air around it. "Follow the movement of the air; either with it or against it does not matter. You just need to move," she continued.

Jael could feel her body separate as Salima ran through her, so she followed the flow of the moving air. As she moved faster, she could feel her body pulling itself tighter together. The faster she went the more compact she became.

"You did it, Jael!" yelled Salima, watching Jael speed away on a tendril of smoke. "Now, slow down and think of where you want your body to materialize then stop moving the energy around your body," Salima told her.

Slowing her speed, Jael thought of the clear spot in front of Salima. When she got there, she stopped focusing on moving her body's energy. The smoke lost its form, and Jael ended up in a heap on the ground in front of Salima.

"That was fantastic. We just need to work on those landings." Salima laughed.

"I can't wait to show Sarik." She giggled while Salima helped her off the ground.

"If only your training with Tal could go so well," Salima commented.

Seriousness now replaced the smile on Jael's face. She dusted off her skirt and asked, "Do you know when the party from Hem is supposed to arrive?"

Pursing her lips as she thought, Salima answered, "I believe I heard Tam say they expected them back this afternoon. He and Lenni argued about it earlier."

"I'm not surprised." She shook her head. "Telling Lenni she can't do something is like telling Halis to stop talking." Jael laughed as the two of them began the long walk out of the woods.

"You know your powers are useless against other Jinn, so it's important you learn to defend yourself without the use of your powers." Salima told her not letting Jael avoid the subject. "Today is my last day training you. Starting tomorrow you will meet with Tal."

Jael frowned and rolled her eyes. She hated the idea and so did every bone in her soon to be bruised body.

Salima laughed at Jael's expression. "Don't worry, you'll get used to the bumps and bruises."

"She almost killed me last time," complained Jael.

"Well, now that you can heal yourself quite rapidly, a few knife wounds shouldn't be a problem."

"But they still hurt like hell."

"And that's something you need to work through. Pain is a distraction if you don't learn to block it out." They stopped walking and Salima eyed Jael.

"Easier said than done," groaned Jael.

"I do have one move I can show you. Now, this only works if you are close enough to put both hands on the person at one time. Okay, grab me from behind. Put your arm around my neck in a chokehold and do your best to block my powers completely. Let me know when you are ready."

Jael did as Salima said and choked her from behind. "Alright, I'm re—" She was unable to finish her sentence before crumbling to the ground in excruciating pain.

"Jael, are you okay?" asked Salima, standing over her.

"Ow. What the hell was that?" Jael moaned, curled up in the fetal position.

"That's called using a person's body as a conduit by passing large amounts of energy from one hand to the other," she replied, helping Jael up from the ground.

"How do I form the energy?"

"Excite the energy that's already in your body and push it out of one hand and into the other through the other person's body. You have to be careful that you have both hands on them; otherwise, all you will do is drain your own energy. So, I want you to put your palms together in front of you and move the energy through your body from one hand to the other and back around like a circle," Salima explained as they began to walk again.

"Like this?" asked Jael, her hands palm to palm, fingers pointing straight up.

"Yes. Do you feel the energy flowing?"

"Yes."

"Remember the faster you move that energy, the more it will hurt the other person when it goes through," Salima added, before shushing Jael's response and cocking her head to the side to listen.

Salima stopped walking. She heard the sound of animals rustling in the woods, so she reached out to them mentally. It was the pack of wolves Tal had joined with on the road from Harwell. Peering into their minds, she could see the message they had for her. *The army moves* relayed one of the wolves, showing Salima what he had seen. Well-armed men traveled hidden from sight within the mist along the border of Eir. Retreating from the wolf's mind, Salima grabbed Jael by the arm. "We must hurry," was all she said before turning to a wisp of smoke and disappearing towards the house.

Seconds later Jael followed rematerializing near the house and just like last time, splayed across the ground.

Salima was already talking with Sarik and Tam when Jael peeled herself off the ground and joined them.

"Are you sure their army is on the move?" asked Sarik.

"I'm certain. They have at least one Jinn hiding them in a heavy fog," Salima told him.

"Tam, we need to get our men on the border. I'll contact Captain Ross and have him return from Hem immediately. We'll need the extra shuttle on the border too," said Sarik.

Running his hand down his face, Tam sighed. "The men are far from ready to do combat, Sarik. You and I both know that."

"We have little choice. At least we have three Jinn and two Nauss on our side, plus the shuttles feeding us intel. If worse comes to worst, we'll burn the forest down around them before they have a chance to engage in battle," Sarik suggested.

"If you're going to move troops, you'd better do it soon. We're about to lose daylight," Salima pointed out.

"Tam, go ahead with your men to the forest near the lake and take Var with you. Tal and Fairen are there and will coordinate their men with yours. Salima and I will take the rest to the area just east of Annoc and see if we can't surprise them from the rear," explained Sarik.

Clearing her throat to get Sarik's attention, Jael asked, "And who am I to go with?"

They all looked at her before Sarik finally responded, "You're staying where you are. I can't chance anything happening to you. Besides, during combat you'd be a liability to me. I wouldn't be able to concentrate on what I need to do if I'm worried about keeping you safe."

Arms crossed, Jael retorted, "I did not spend the last week training just to be left behind. You need me, Sarik. Like you said, we have three Jinn, and if I'm not mistaken you counted me in that number."

"The answer is no, Jael, and that's final," he commanded.

Before he was done speaking, she turned into wisp of smoke and moved swiftly towards the woods. Sarik snapped his fingers in front of him and created an energy wall before her. As soon as Jael smashed into it she rematerialized in a heap on the ground moaning in pain. Sarik walked over and put out his hand to help her up.

"You're not ready," he said softly as he helped her off the ground. "You have no idea what it's like to battle another Jinn—or, in my case, a Nauss."

"Sarik, I need to help you get my mother's necklace. Just let me go with you as far as the lake and help there. If things get too heated, the shuttle can pick me up in the nearby meadow," she pleaded.

Searching for a reason to say no, Sarik took his time responding. "Very well. But only because I worry you might go out on your own if I leave you here. God forbid you should listen to me," he grumbled, giving in to her request against his better judgment.

"Be ready to go in ten minutes, or I'll leave you here," he stated, still looking for a reason to leave her behind.

"I'll be ready in five," she volleyed back as she headed towards the house.

~~

It was almost dawn by the time Tam's men made it to the lake. Tal and Fairen waited for them at the edge of the camp. Breakfast was already made in preparation of their arrival and by the time Tam's men were done eating, Fairen's were awake and their tents were empty for Tam's men to rest.

Having made it back from Hem, Captain Ross scanned the forests from above. The shuttle remained unseen by either side, a requirement by Nauss directives. It was unfortunate intel was all he could provide. *The shuttle had enough fire power to end this skirmish swiftly*, he thought. He made pass after pass looking meticulously for Haro's men in the forest. After a couple of high level flybys, he hovered the shuttle and scanned within areas of dense fog. Before long he was able to ascertain the location and number of Haro's men and passed that on to Sarik.

Once contacted by Captain Ross, Sarik called a meeting to discuss options for ending the battle between them and Haro.

"I have word that about two hundred of Haro's men are in the forest just over the hill there on the other side of the lake," Sarik said, pointing to a hill on the morning horizon shrouded in dense fog. "Haro can't keep this fog up forever, and now that the sun is coming up, he'll have a hard time keeping a heavy fog in place. However, we need to wait for the fog to lift before making any moves."

"Do we know what kind of weapons they carry?" asked Kale

"Not yet. Captain Ross is working from high altitudes, as per orders from Hy-Brasil which prevent him from getting closer look. Unless there is a valid reason, such as unauthorized weapons, he cannot break the directive," explained Sarik.

"I've tried to make contact with some of the wildlife, but everything is just outside my reach—like he cleared the forest before we got here. We do have the wolf pack that followed, but they're resting now," informed Salima.

"I just contacted the second shuttle. They're telling me that Haro's camp is fairly empty, with around thirty men or so left. There was a large group that went north and ran into Leif's army, mostly defectors seeking asylum," reported Tal.

"It sounds like we're only facing the two hundred in the forest. Hopefully they mostly consist of men who are just fearful to leave Haro's service. Once they realize he's no longer a threat, I'm sure they'll be quick to surrender," theorized Sarik.

"I hope you're right. I would hate for my soldiers to cut down men who are only fighting because of fear and not because they believed what they were doing was righteous." Fairen sighed before joining his men.

By noon, the fog had lifted, leaving Haro's men vulnerable, but Sarik forbade any of his men to engage in what would be an all-out slaughter. Instead, he opted to try and take out Haro in a precision strike.

After they were rested, Sarik had his men move to the right and Tam's men move to the left. Fairen's more experienced men would engage them from the front and divert their attention. Once to their back side, Tam and his men would herd Haro's soldiers from the back, leaving Salima, Tal and himself to take care of Haro and the remaining men at his camp. The quicker they could take him down the better

Sarik relayed his plan to the others, and they waited for an opportune time to strike. Jael had plans of her own. She would wisp in and grab the necklace before Haro knew what hit him. It was the only way Jael could stop the information in the necklace from getting to Sarik's men and the entire clan.

As soon as Sarik and his men were gone, Jael turned into a wisp of smoke and traveled to Haro's camp. However, Sarik forgot his sword and came back to camp for it. It didn't take him long to discover Jael was missing.

Sarik screamed, furious with Jael. If Haro didn't kill her, he would. He grabbed his sword and joined his men in the forest. The new plan was simple: storm the camp and save Jael.

Chapter 16

Jael moved through Haro's camp swiftly on the air, but as soon as she reached his tent she lost her mist form and rematerialized. She threw open the flap and marched inside, determined to put an end to all the fighting and retrieve her mother's necklace. She looked around the large tent and spotted Wren laid out on a pile of pillows on top one of the many carpets that covered the floor.

Surprised to see Jael, Wren got up from the ground and walked over to her sister. "Death cannot come soon enough for you," she spat through gritted teeth.

"Now, now, Wren, is that any way to speak to our guest?" boomed a voice from behind Jael, startling her. "Come in and have a drink with me," he sang, clasping his hand tightly around Jael's arm and pulling her into the tent. He pushed her onto the pile of pillows Wren had just got up from.

"Cut the crap, Haro. I know you're a Jinn," Jael hissed, adjusting herself on the pillows.

"Smart girl," he said, his mouth pulling up on one side in a sadistic grin.

"Haro, just be done with her." Wren's venomous remark left a chill down Jael's spine.

"Why do you hate me?" Jael questioned, her demeanor softening from its agitated state.

"I'm the oldest. I should be Lady of Eir. You and Sarik have taken everything from me!" she yelled.

"It was not my choice to make," stated Jael in a low voice.

"Lies!"

In a burst of rage, Jael balled her fists and went on the offense. "Father was the one who arranged my marriage. I'm the one who should be angry at you, Wren. You were given the chance to be Lady of Eir. All you had to do is marry Tam, but instead you married that arrogant oaf, Dugun. So don't sit here and accuse me of ruining your life when you have done this all to yourself," Jael shouted back.

Standing quickly from his throne-like chair, Haro boomed out like a god from the heavens. "Enough! Silence yourself, Wren, or I'll do it for you," he said, ending their argument. He walked over to a long narrow table and poured two glasses of liquor. He handed one to Jael then sat back down in his chair with the other.

Jael fingered the glass. It was from Hy-Brasil, and judging from looks of the cushions and rugs, they were too.

Light played hide and seek with Wren's see-through gown as she sat on Haro's lap, giving Jael a smug grin before kissing him. Disgusted, Jael turned her head and downed her glass of liquor. The drink burned her throat, but warmed her body. She wanted to leave, but lacked the courage to do so.

Jael ignored them and looked for the box which contained her mother's necklace. As she scanned the room, she noticed a jeweled dagger on a small table next to Haro and behind it a box with Nauss writing on it. Wren turned and straddled Haro. Soon they were both enthralled with each other and neither paid attention to Jael.

She crept along the tent wall behind Haro's chair and reached out for the box. A loud ruckus from outside startled Haro, and he pushed Wren off his lap and reached for his dagger. He noticed Jael's hand reaching out for the box, and he quickly grabbed her arm. He pulled her in front of him and held the knife to her throat.

Sarik burst into Haro's tent with Salima and Tal on his heels. But when he saw Haro's hostage, he stopped dead in his tracks.

"You can't win, Sarik," proclaimed Haro, tightening his grip on Jael.

"Let her go. She has nothing to do with this." Sarik didn't move a muscle for fear that Haro would kill Jael.

Haro gave a deep sinister laugh then flames danced within his eyes. "That's where you're wrong. This has everything to do with Jael. She belongs to me. I created her to serve me," he bellowed as a small trickle of blood dripped down Jael's neck. "Tell him who I really am, Salima," he said before he changed into a beautiful woman with long flowing black hair, her skin as blue as the noon sky and the eyes of a cat.

"Kali," Salima whispered under her breath, before speaking aloud. "Kali, stop this madness," she pleaded. "You're a Jinn and this is not our way!"

"You think I'm like you?" she laughed. "I'm Nephilim, not Jinn!" she boomed.

"Who are the Nephilim?" asked Jael, relaxing her body hoping to distract Kali.

For a second, Kali loosened her grip on Jael. "Let's just say, we're the Jinn's dirty little secret," she shrugged.

Salima wanted to buy Sarik some time and explained. "The Nephilim are a race of warriors who once served the Veshtu. They were the keepers of man when the Veshtu left Earth to cull other planets. During the Veshtu's long absences, the Nephilim corrupted men and gave them the ability to reason, causing them to turn on the Veshtu. Angered by this, the Nephilim were cast out by the Veshtu and forbidden to return to Earth. They're the demons of our race," Salima spat.

A sinister half grin crept up Kali's face. "But the Veshtu could not stop us from returning if we wanted too. The Nephilim look so much like the peaceful Jinn that the Veshtu take their anger out on them instead," she laughed. "When a Nephil choses to make havoc they come here and entice men to do evil, just for the sake of causing chaos. We are the demons men fear."

"Why were my mother's records marked *Origin*?" Jael asked, remembering her and Salima's trip to the Jinn charter house.

"Because, my pretty, I'm the origin of the DNA. I replaced your mother's with my own combined with your father's. The funny thing about that is, I didn't even get the idea until after I lay with your father," Kali disclosed, tightening her grip once more. "You were supposed to stay in Atlantis, but your mother feared you would be taken from her and rightfully so. I always planned on taking you, but then I was forced to leave Atlantis by King Varen when he found out my plan. He and Salima have been protecting you for the last eighteen years, not that Salima had a clue I was the one that she protected you from." She smirked.

Tears welled up in Jael's eyes as she grasped what Kali was saying. She was not Jinn, but a Nephil—a demon. It was like the world was crashing down. Her whole life had been a lie perpetuated by secrets. The stunned look on Sarik's face said it all and death seemed a kinder outcome than losing Sarik's love, so she mustered up the courage she lacked earlier and made her move.

Placing her hand on each side of Kali, Jael forced the energy in her body to go out one hand through Kali and into the other. As pain wracked through Kali's body, the knife plunged deeply into Jael's throat.

Stunned, Sarik couldn't believe what just happened. When it sank in, he ran to Jael screaming, "No!" As he knelt next to her, Tal and Salima seized Kali and Wren screamed hysterically in the background.

Frantically, Sarik struggled to stop Jael from bleeding out. He wove the cells back together as quickly as he could, starting with her jugular. He mentally mended her wound, touching his mind to hers. He felt her attempting to stop the bleeding herself until unconsciousness overtook her.

Sarik yelled, "I need help!"

Within seconds Var entered the tent and helped Sarik mend all the blood vessels that had been cut. The bleeding stopped, and Sarik breathed a sigh of relief when he could still feel Jael's faint pulse under his fingers. He sat in the pool of blood that covered the floor and held her body close to his watching each and every ragged breath.

Tam entered the tent to tell Sarik the good news, the battle was over with little injury, but when he saw the blood covered Sarik clutching Jael, he became sickened and left the tent. His news could wait until later.

It was noon before anyone was brave enough to enter the tent again. Sarik had not moved in an hour, and everyone worried for their king and queen. This time Tam was prepared for the bloodbath when he entered. Walking over to Sarik, he gently put a hand on his shoulder and spoke, "Sarik, we need to move Jael to the shuttle. She can be looked after better in Atlantis."

Salima and Var peeked into the tent while Tam spoke to Sarik. When they saw Sarik nod, they grabbed the gurney and entered the tent. Gently they moved Jael onto the gurney then turned on the anti-gravity, so it would be a smooth ride to the shuttle. No one cared if their secret was found out. They would either accept what Jael and Sarik were or lose the two people who could hold this new kingdom together.

Boarding the shuttle after Jael, Sarik sat somberly next to her. Griping her hand, he wept quietly. He reached out mentally, but her life force was no longer there and an inconsolable emptiness filled him—one that could never be mended by anyone else.

Captain Ross piloted the shuttle to a landing area where a medical team was waiting for their arrival. They rushed onto the shuttle and whisked Jael away, leaving Sarik behind.

Varen watched as the team flew pass him, and Sarik mindlessly exited the shuttle. When he reached out to his son, his mind was flooded with all of Sarik's too familiar gutted emotions. They reminded Varen of how he felt when Sarik's mother died, and he staggered back before regaining his own cognizance. He followed Sarik into the large ground ship that followed the medical transport. "They're going to put her in stasis. There's still a chance she'll make it. It's just going to take time."

Letting out a loud growl, Sarik punched the inside wall of the ship repeatedly. Varen winced as Sarik's pain ripped through him in an uncontrollable rage. He threw his arm around his son and held him tight until his fury ebbed.

"Sarik, you have to stay strong for her. For her people," he whispered with all the worry of a loving parent.

The ship stopped, and Sarik was swiftly escorted to the stasis department by the technicians waiting for him at the door. As soon as he stepped inside the doctors all glanced up at him from Jael's pod. Their worried looks gave Sarik an ominous feeling. He looked inside her pod which made her skin shimmer in the blue glow.

I've got to pull myself together. She'll need as much positive energy as I can muster, he thought before addressing the doctors.

"I hope you have good news for me," he said without emotion.

"Your highness, she's still hanging on. Our problem is her blood is like nothing we have ever seen. A transfusion is impossible. We've tried to replicate the blood cells inside her body, but it was too complicated. I've sent her blood profile to be replicated by the lab, but it'll take time," replied one of the doctors.

"Is there anything I can do to help?" Sarik asked, relieved there was still hope.

"There's nothing you can do for her. You should go home and rest while you can. I'll keep you updated if anything changes," he said.

Sarik thanked the doctors as they left the room. He placed his hands on the pod and reached out to her one last time with his mind, but still found nothing. Salima waited for him in the hall.

"How are you holding up?" she asked.

"I've been better," he replied with a small ingenuine chuckle as he ran his fingers through his hair.

She gave him a lopsided concerned grin then placed her hand on his shoulder. "Do you want to talk about it?"

He looked at Salima with tear filled eyes and nodded. "But not here."

Opening the door to his quarters, Sarik inhaled deeply. Jael's scent of lavender still lingered in the stale air. He flipped the switch to the fire pit and plopped down on the couch. Sitting across from him, Salima took a good look at Sarik's worried expression. She tried to read what was going on, but he kept his emotions well-guarded.

"They have bonded Kali and plan to have her shipped to Enadlon within the week," she relayed.

"I know that should make me feel better, but it doesn't. I'm a monster, Salima. The moment Jael saw my shocked expression it was all over. I didn't even have the chance to explain, and now she's lying in a stasis pod for who knows how long, thinking that she's an abomination. I did that

Salima, not Kali!" he spat, the vein in his neck visibly pulsing to his anger.

"It was a mistake, a misunderstanding. That's not your fault, Sarik," she said in an attempt to console him.

"I don't know what in the hell is happening to me. I can't decide if I want to hit something or cry," he admitted to her.

Salima got up from her seat and sat next to him. Turning sideways, she put her arms around him in a motherly embrace. She shuddered as Sarik let down his guard and his emotions flooded her mind. It was much more than guilt consuming him. Fear, anger, confusion and love all left their marks on his weary mind. He sobbed on her shoulder. After a few minutes, he sucked in a deep breath and let it out, ending his tears.

"Look at me, Salima. I'm turning into a sniveling woman." He chuckled, wiping his face with his sleeve.

"I think you've never had your heart broken before," she pointed out.

"I didn't know falling in love also meant losing your dignity," he snorted, standing up and stepping into the kitchen. He rinsed his face and dried it, throwing the dampened towel on the counter. Seconds later the door chimed. Sarik gave Salima an exasperated look, so she got up and answered the door for him, ready to turn away all visitors. She looked at the door panel and saw it was Varen. "It's you dad," she said, waiting for a reply from Sarik.

"Let him in," he said before sitting at the kitchen table.

She opened the door and let Varen in. Before he saw Sarik, he said, "I came to check on my son."

She pointed him in the direction of the kitchen. "How are you holding up, son?" he asked, but he already knew the answer to that question by the appearance of red swollen eyes and frown on his face.

"How did you do it? How did you keep from falling apart when mom died?"

"I didn't. For a while I went completely mad. Then one day I woke up, and this tiny face greeted me with eyes just like his mother's. It was the moment I realized the gift your mother left me with, and I knew she would always be with me."

Sarik had a new found respect for his father. Jael was still alive and not completely lost to him like his mother. But now he understood his father's pain and the strength he must have had to raise a child on his own after his loss. They talked for a couple of hours, but the long day and emotional stress left Sarik exhausted. He took a hot shower and climbed into bed, quickly falling into a peaceful slumber.

~~~

The icy wind ate into his skin. It was colder than usual, and Sarik began to rethink his decision to walk to the hospital. Jael's condition had not changed in three days. The doctors tried transfusing the blood that had been replicated in the lab, but were unsuccessful which left them scratching their heads. Too lost in thought to produce heat, Sarik shivered and pulled his jacket tighter around his chest. A transport pulled up beside him and Tam opened the door.

"What in the world are you doing here?" Sarik questioned before entering the transport.

"I came to check on our illustrious leader and his wife. Plus I have news," said Tam.

"Please tell me it's good news."

Wrinkling his nose, Tam sighed. "Well, not exactly. Wren is still missing. Even the shuttles haven't been able to locate her, and we found Betta. It appears Kali killed her two years ago and cast a glamor on their housemaid to look like her. It would explain Betta's odd behavior when Lenni was visiting them last year. She said it was like talking to a stranger."

"Why would Kali kill her?" he asked, furrowing his brow.

"According to her replacement, Betta was wise to Haro's plans, and unlike Wren, she refused to go along with them. How's Jael?"

"No change. The doctors want to discuss a new treatment strategy today. I hope they have figured out something. This has been the longest three days of my life," Sarik grumbled.

"I'm sorry to hear that. If it's any consolation, the clans are doing great. Leif has taken command of Canulis, and the clan is getting back to normal. My father has finally decided to lend me a hand with running Eir, which I'm very grateful for. He's already making plans with the other clans for the summer solstice."

"That's fantastic. I know I left in a hurry, so it's good to hear you and Leif can run things without me."

"Nonetheless, we're all wondering when you'll return?" questioned Tam, just as the transport pulled up to the hospital.

Stepping out, Sarik responded, "I'm not coming back without Jael."

Not wanting to argue, Tam quietly followed Sarik to the stasis room. When they got there, Sarik balled his hands into fists ready to strike the man who was leaning against Jael's pod. His hair so pale it was almost was almost white. Ice blue eyes and a lithe body, there was no doubt he was a Veshtu. Before Sarik could get to him, a young, beautiful woman stepped between them. Her hair looked like the fall leaves glistening in the sun with strands of gold sparkling randomly throughout. Deep green eyes with dark lashes and a perfect up-turned nose perched above her lips. But the one feature that got Sarik's attention was her slightly pointed ears—a trait exclusive to Nauss royalty. Stunned, Sarik gawked at them until his father interrupted his stupor.

"Sarik, this is Io and Nilus. They're here to help," his father said.

"But he is a Veshtu!" exclaimed Sarik, hands still fisted.

"He and Io are married, both exiled for their love. They're here to help Jael and do so at a great risk to themselves. Nilus is one of the leading genetic scientists when it comes to human/alien blood. He helped create homosapians," Varen explained.

Sarik relaxed his hands. He knew the tale of the wayward lovers before him. It was an age old legend of star crossed lovers and forbidden love—one his people knew well and were not soon to forget. He walked over and extended his hand to Nilus.

"My apologies. Please forgive my ignorance," he said, shaking Nilus' hand.

"Accepted–now let's get down to business. I've pulled all the labs and genetic data. It appears her blood is transforming rapidly, something common to Jinn juveniles as they become adult. Every time your scientists try to introduce replicated blood into her system, she rejects it because her blood no longer matches. The only way to rectify this problem is to transfuse her with her mother's blood," Nilus explained.

Sarik's face went white as he looked to his dad then bolted out the door yelling something about the ship leaving.

"Damn it!" exclaimed Varen, pressing his communicator button. "I want the airfield locked down now! Nothing gets out of that spaceport until I personally say it does. Now, patch me to Captain Lore."

"Is there a problem?" asked Nilus.

"Jael's genetic donor is on a ship due to leave for Enadlon any minute. Hello, Captain Lore?"

"Yes, and this damn well better be important, I'm about to miss my take off window," said the man on the other end of the com link.

Varen breathed a sigh of relief then replied, "I'm sending the medics and security to retrieve Kali. Consider the flight canceled until further notice."

"It looks like security is already here," he said before disconnecting.

"Sarik must have called security," Varen commented. "Had they taken off, it could be days before they would have been able to land again."

Soon the medics returned with blood from Kali. Nilus carefully transfused Jael while Io monitored her body for rejection. Sarik loomed over Jael like a hawk as Tam and Varen observed from the corner of the room. After several minutes without change, Sarik started to get antsy. He carefully probed Jael's mind looking for any semblance of life. Just as he was about to give up, he felt warmth surround him like a blanket as Jael's mind awoke from its slumber. Her confused emotions were like being pulled underwater and unable to breathe. He reached out to comfort her. *I'm here, Jael, I'll always be here.*

~~~

Gasping for air, Jael inhaled deeply and opened her eyes. Sarik stood over her clutching her hand. His smile contradicted his tear filled eyes. Remembering her last moments, Jael put her hand on her neck, feeling for the wound Kali left. Looking around she knew she was in Atlantis, she closed her eyes and sighed feeling Sarik's love infiltrating her mind. *I must be dreaming*, she thought, embracing him with all of her being.

This is no dream, my love. He lightly touched her cheek then brought the hand he was clasping up to his lips and kissed her fingertips.

Epilogue

No longer guised with old age, Jael and Sarik stood on the flight line awaiting the release of the last mooring clamp in preparation for the Atlantis' departure later that day. They lived out their human lives in Eirland and now settled in for their immortal one on the Atlantis.

"Sarik, do you think it is wise to leave him here?" asked Jael.

He put his arm around her waist and watched at the last of the shuttles leave for the Valhalla. "He's not a baby anymore, Jael. You need to let him be a man and some time away from his mother will do him good."

She sighed and leaned her head against his chest. "I know he's a grown man, but this is Aidan we're talking about. He's a bit of a handful—just like someone else I know," she added, nudging him with her elbow.

"I'm sure his uncle Odin will keep him in check. However, he's just embracing his nickname to its entirety." Sarik laughed.

Rolling her eyes, she looked up at Sarik and chuckled. "And you don't think I should worry that they call him Loki? Does that not mean trickster in your language?"

"Yes, it does. But could you expect anything less from child with the name of Aidan Alexander Rowe Poseidon." He smiled, leaned over, and kissed her.

Before he released her from his kiss, Jael reached around and firmly grabbed his backside pulling him hard against her.

He softly growled when she nipped the bottom of his lip as he pulled away. Jael ran her tongue up the side of his neck until she reached his ear.

"Want to play kiss and beg?" she whispered.

Excitement coursed through him as Jael's hot breath breezed across the skin of his neck. "I'd love too. Although I'm certain I'll do all the begging." He laughed, flagging down a transport to take them home.

As a teen C.G. Powell was selected as a member of her school's newspaper staff. After her first article the editor decided the darkroom was a more suitable place for her skills…or lack of. Since then, she has traveled everywhere—thanks to her innate curiosity about the world and the Navy. In her life time, she has learned: aviation electronics, CCNA networking, Gemology and how to get bloodstains out of the carpet (you never know when you might need that). But her latest, all-consuming, endeavor is storytelling. When asked why, her response was "I live to challenge myself; I like to be pushed outside of my comfort zone and writing is one of those things that pushes my boundaries. Besides it was the only way to share all of the crap bouncing around in my head!"

http://www.facebook.com/#!/ChristineGPowell
Blog: http://spellcheckedbycgpowell.blogspot.com/
Christinegpowell@gmail.com

www.ingramcontent.com/pod-product-compliance
Lightning Source LLC
Chambersburg PA
CBHW061322200626
46813CB00017B/2809